THE DARK AND DEADLY POOL

Also by Joan Lowery Nixon

THE GHOSTS OF NOW
THE OTHER SIDE OF DARK
THE SPECTER
THE STALKER

THE DARK AND DEADLY POOL

JOAN LOWERY NIXON

DELACORTE PRESS/NEW YORK

Published by
Delacorte Press
1 Dag Hammarskjold Plaza
New York, New York 10017

MANUFACTURED IN THE UNITED STATES OF AMERICA

FIRST PRINTING

Library of Congress Cataloging in Publication Data
Nixon, Joan Lowery.
The dark and deadly pool.
Summary: Sixteen-year-old Mary Elizabeth's summer job
at an expensive health club turns out to be more exciting
than she bargained for when a series of mysterious events
culminate in murder.
[1. Mystery and detective stories] I. Title.
PZ7.N65Dar 1987   [Fic]   87-6723
ISBN 0-385-29585-5

*For Eileen
with love*

THE DARK
AND DEADLY
POOL

1

Moonlight drizzled down the wide glass wall that touched the surface of the hotel swimming pool, dividing it into two parts. The wind-flicked waters of the outer pool glittered with reflected pin-lights from the moon and stars, but the silent water in the indoor section had been sucked into the blackness of the room.

I blinked, trying to adjust my eyes to the darkness, trying to see the edge of the pool that curved near my feet. I pressed my back against the wall and forced myself to breathe evenly. I whispered aloud, "Mary Elizabeth Rafferty, there is nothing to be afraid of here! Nothing!" But even the sound of my own wobbly words terrified me.

I remembered how glad I'd been to get this summer replacement job at the Ridley Hotel health club. The Ridley is one of those super-beautiful hotels with fresh flowers in silver urns on all their gigantic carved tables and sideboards, and paintings that are the real thing, and a whole collection of sterling pieces which they plan to use if the President ever stays there, which so far he hasn't.

Their health club was designed by an interior decorator in coral and green with loads of looming ficus trees and palms, and white-blossomed "closet plants," and giant-leaved philodendron—all in huge brass planters—which right away tells you that nobody really goes there to get healthy. There's a small room with weight equipment; separate dressing rooms for men and women, with a large sauna in each; a bubbling Jacuzzi; and the pool, which is magnificent. Even though the salary wasn't anything to cheer about, I eagerly agreed to five days a week of scrubbing the tiles around the pool, manning the desk in the health-club office, and keeping a sharp eye through the office window-wall on the swimmers in the indoor section of the pool.

As Mom told me, it was the perfect job for someone who had grown too tall too fast and had been politely dismissed from her first summer job at a hamburger chain because she knocked over too many filled glasses of cola and stumbled over too many table legs.

And, as usual, Mom was right. During the three days I'd been working at the health club, no one seemed to pay attention to a little clumsiness—except for the first day on duty when I fell into the swimming pool—but let's not talk about that. And so far no one here had asked me if I played basketball or what the weather was like "up there" or if I got my red hair from being so close to the sun. At least, here at the health club I wasn't made to feel like an ungainly klutz.

"What you need is confidence in yourself," Dad had said. "A summer job should help you gain confidence."

"We hope it will help you learn to appreciate yourself," Mom had wistfully added. "Mary Elizabeth, you have got to begin to think good, positive things about yourself. Concentrate on all your best qualities."

"That's a blank," I said.

Dad put an arm around my shoulders. "You're a wonderful girl, and the world is filled with wonderful things for you. Just concentrate on what you can put into life and what you want from it."

"What *do* you want?" Mom asked.

"A tall boyfriend," I said flippantly. I wasn't going to tell them what I dreamed of being someday. It was an impossible dream. For that matter, I supposed that a tall boyfriend was too. I thought about some of the tall guys I knew at school. They were all dating girls who were under five feet two. "Might as well make him handsome, while you're at it," I added.

Mom sighed and began to say, "Be serious. You don't understand what we're trying to—"

But Dad held up a hand and said, "All right, sweetheart. If that's what you want right now, keep your goal in mind and don't settle for less." He kissed the end of my nose. "We're proud of you. Good luck with your new job."

I may have flubbed the first job, but here I was with a second-chance five-day-a-week job that lasted from three in the afternoon until eleven at night, when the health club closed.

It was a good job, and I liked it, with one exception: those few terrifying minutes at closing when I was alone in that echoing, cavernous room with the dark, lonely pool.

The first two nights I had to shoo out a few dawdling guests—politely, of course. Then I checked both the men's and women's dressing rooms to make sure everyone had left, locked the door to the outside deck, and turned out the pool lights and club lights in the office. In the dark I secured the office door with a loud click that shuddered through the steamy silence, then trembled across the twenty feet between the office door and the door to the corridor leading from the club to the side lobby of the hotel. I frantically slammed and locked the large door to the health club, grateful to be out in the brightly lit corridor, glad to be leaving that humid, watery darkness, and thankful that no one had heard those little gasping noises I'd been making. I couldn't help feeling ashamed that I was behaving not like a sixteen-year-old with my first *real* job, but like a child who was afraid of being alone in the dark.

I knew I had to grow up, and the only way to do it was to conquer this childish fear. So on this, the third night at work, I deliberately waited outside the locked office door, next to the dark pool. I pressed my back against the cold rough-textured wall and quietly willed myself to relax. I squeezed my eyes shut while I took two deep breaths. It worked! My breathing slowed, and my shoulders relaxed against the wall. But droplets of sweat trickled down my backbone, and my bare legs were clammy from the humidity in the room.

As I waited, shapes crept out of shadows and became familiar patio chairs and tables and potted palms and ferns. Shining tiles edged the pool, and the surface of the black water gleamed like polished jet stone.

I had to smile. It wasn't so bad here in the dark. This room was a crazy place in which to be alone, but I could manage. I was proud of myself. I would never let that unreasonable fear get to me again.

When I heard the splash outside I first thought it must be my imagination. It was a small noise, not the wild splashing the kids made, and certainly not the loud belly-flopping splash caused by some of the overweight hotel conventioneers who were under the impression they were diving. I listened carefully and stared into the darkness, stepping to the very edge of the pool.

A shadow at the bottom of the pool, blacker than the dark water above it, slipped under the glass divider and quivered in my direction like a shimmer of lightning. I watched it come, too terrified to move, too frightened to scream, as the shadow loomed upward, ripping the water. Hands clutched at the edge of the pool, one of them grabbing the toe of my sneaker, which was in the way; and a face—eyes and mouth gaping and gasping—met my own.

I screamed, and an echoing scream came from the mouth below mine. With a loud gulp of air and thrashing of water, the face disappeared under the dark surface. I could see the shadow quickly slip under the glass wall and enter the outside part of the pool.

I stumbled and tripped to the office door, dropping the keys. Somehow I managed to find them, get the door open, and turn on the office light. Sprawling across the desk, I grabbed the telephone and rang the hotel's security office number.

"Yo," a deep voice answered.

I couldn't mistake the voice. It came from Lamar Boudry, Ridley chief of security, who styled himself a Symbol of Controlled Confidence and who periodically roamed through the corridors and lobby of the hotel like a marked patrol car. His impressive appearance in black, from his tightly cropped hair and moustache down to his shining black shoes with elevator heels, silently informed the guests they could retire with ease, knowing they were well protected at the Ridley Hotel.

"Mr. Boudry," I shouted, "it's me, Liz Rafferty! Help me! There's someone in the swimming pool!"

"Tell him it's closing time, and he's got to get out." Lamar Boudry yawned loudly into the phone and my ear.

"I can't tell him anything! He grabbed my foot, screamed in my face, and disappeared under the water!"

"Can you describe him? Did he have webbed fingers or green fangs?"

"I'm not kidding, Mr. Boudry! Come and help me!"

"I've got both the inside and outside pool area on camera right now, Liz, and I don't see anyone there, except you in the office."

"But outside—"

"Nobody's outside. Place is empty."

"Somebody must have sneaked in!"

"No way to get over those walls." He yawned again. "I saw you turn off the lights in the club ten minutes ago. How come you're still hanging around there?"

"Well, I—that is, I wanted to get over being scared in the dark, and I—" I stopped and took a deep breath. "Let me start over. It sounds like—"

"It sounds like you've got a big imagination. Maybe the hotel should get you a night-light."

"Mr. Boudry! Aren't you even going to come down here and look?"

"I'm looking, I'm looking. That's what these monitors are for. Why don't you just lock up now and go on home?"

"No!" I thumped a fist on the desk and managed to upset a jar of pens and pencils, which rolled off the desk and over the floor. "Whoever was in the pool might be hiding somewhere around here, and I can't lock up the club with him in it!"

"Okay, okay," Boudry drawled. "Tina hasn't checked out yet. I'll send her down to look around. And I'll keep an eye on the area through the cameras."

"Thanks," I mumbled, and hung up. I flipped on all the switches, so that the entire area—inside and outside—was colored in intense artificial light. The pool became a bright-blue jewel. The trees and shrubs that rimmed the outside tiles dripped in lemon-green. With the black sky beyond, the club resembled one of those garish paintings on black velvet that were sold on vacant lots along Highway 6 and Westheimer.

The door to the club swung open and Tina called out, "Help has arrived. Where are you, Liz?"

I skidded across the pencils, managing to steady myself by hanging onto the door frame as I swung out of the office to face Tina Martinez.

Tina's dark hair was cut short and straight, in line with Boudry's regulations for security personnel, but Tina filled out her uniform of white shirt, maroon jacket, and slacks so well that her hair was not the first thing people noticed about her. When Tina was my age she had worked at the hotel health club, but this summer she was nineteen and had been hired for a full-time position with security. "She nagged me into hiring her," Boudry told everyone, but he let everyone know that Tina was good at her job.

According to Tina, however, her mind was set on higher things. She'd enrolled in a couple of summer college courses and was going to work and study her way eventually into a master's degree in psychology. At least then she could analyze everyone legally. Legal or not, I'd never met anyone so full of advice.

As I regained my balance, Tina tried to peer around me. "Somebody chasing you, or what?" she asked.

I shook the hair from my eyes. "No, no. He was in the pool." I told Tina what had happened.

"What did he look like?"

"I don't know. It was dark, and I was scared. Tina, it all happened in just a few seconds!"

"Records show," Tina said, "that most eyewitnesses are not very accurate, so don't worry if you can't give me details. Basically, it's an emotional problem. Your space is threatened, that sort of stuff. It's in all the books." She walked to the glass wall and tried to open the door. "Get your key, Liz. We'll check around outside."

My fingers trembled, but I managed to unlock the door.

The slight breeze was warm and heavy with moisture, yet I realized I was shivering. "What if he's hiding out here somewhere?" I whispered.

While she talked, Tina poked in and under the shrubbery that lined the outer brick wall. "You forget, Liz, you're protected by the Ridley Hotel security force. Our brave leader has put down the espionage novel he was reading to keep us on camera. And I'm here. Did I tell you that I made top scores in my marksmanship test last week?"

"I didn't know you took the test."

Tina scowled at me over her shoulder and mouthed something that I couldn't make out. She gave a final sweeping glance to the pool area, then came over to join me.

"Whoever he was, he's not here," she said. "My guess is that he went over the wall, probably the same way he came in."

"Isn't the wall too high?"

Tina shrugged. "Maybe he's a super athlete. We have to keep our options open." She gave one last glance around. "I don't think there's anything to worry about, and since you lock the door between the club and the hotel, whoever it was couldn't get into the hotel. At least the Symbol of Controlled Confidence and his security staff protect the guests while they're *inside* the hotel." She sighed. "I wish we could do something about protecting them when they're *outside*."

"Protecting them from what?"

Tina lowered her voice. "Don't blab it around, because the hotel is trying to keep a lid on it, and Lamar is having fits about what's happening. A lot of the guests are having their wallets lifted during their first or second day in Houston."

"You mean pickpockets?"

"Right."

"But that could happen to anyone in any city."

"Not in such quantity. Not from one hotel in particular."

"I don't see how the hotel could be involved," I told her.

"None of us can," she said. "That's the trouble."

She led the way back inside and waited while I once again locked the glass door. "You shouldn't have said what you did about the marksmanship test."

"I'm sorry," I told her. "I didn't know about the test."

"There wasn't any test."

"Then what are you talking about?"

"Don't you see? I was psyching him out, in case he was hiding somewhere." Tina smiled. "My theory is that the mind is a more potent weapon than a gun. When I'm a psychologist—"

The telephone rang in the health-club office. I rushed to answer it.

It was Boudry. "Since everything's okay down there, tell Tina to get herself to room 902. Some complaints about a noisy party. Tell her after she's handled that, she can go on home." Before I had a chance to answer, Boudry hung up.

I relayed the message to Tina. I grabbed my handbag and turned off the lights, scrambling to follow Tina out of the health club.

In the corridor Tina turned to face me. "This guy you think you saw in the pool tonight—there's another possibility to consider."

"But I did see him," I began.

Tina interrupted. "Judging by the way you were breathing after you turned out the lights, sort of like the way a fish gasps when he flops around, we could be looking at something deeper."

"What?"

Tina nodded solemnly and said, "Perhaps you saw only a manifestation of your inner fears."

"I did not!" I yelled. "I saw somebody! A person! He screamed at me!"

"You were afraid of the dark when you were little and thought that something lived under your bed. Right?"

That stopped me for a moment, and I stammered, "Well, sure. But who didn't?"

"I didn't," Tina said. "You have unresolved conflicts in your life. Right?"

"But everybody—"

"Be specific. Is there something you'd like to do, but think you can't?"

Immediately a picture came to my eyes. It was the same picture that I liked to dwell on before I fell asleep at night. In the picture I'm standing at the podium in Jones Hall in front of the Houston Symphony Orchestra. I nod to the first violinist, raise my baton, and music swirls and swells to the back row of the top balcony as I once again conduct the orchestra to greatness, fame, and good reviews in the Houston *Post* and *Chronicle.*

But how can a superb conductor not be a superb musician? Over the last few years I've tried piano, guitar, and drums in that order; but Mom kept getting migraine headaches. The band director at school suggested I learn the flute, but every time I practiced at home Dad rushed out to take a walk.

Houston Symphony Orchestra conductor? The only symphonies I'll ever conduct are those in the car, when I tune in KLEF. I didn't like Tina prying into my private dreams. No one knew about them, and she wouldn't either!

I stretched to my full height and yelled down at Tina, "My private life has nothing to do with what I saw in the swimming pool tonight! Someone *was* there, and I saw him!"

"Okay, okay," Tina said. "I'm not a psychologist yet, so we'll handle it your way." She paused. "However—"

"There's a noisy party in Room 902!" I shouted.

"You're kind of a noisy party yourself," Tina said, and giggled.

I couldn't help laughing. I was being pretty huffy. I relaxed a little and said, "I'll see you tomorrow afternoon."

"I'll probably be on camera duty," Tina said. "Give me a call if any good-looking hunks come in."

"I know you. You'll find them before I do," I told her. I followed Tina down the corridor and into the lobby.

As Tina headed for the elevators, I went toward the back of the hotel and out through the employees' checkpoint. I guess all big hotels have a certain amount of theft from employees, but—according to Tina—the Ridley had been having a higher rate than usual. Lamar had set up both rules and equipment. We could take nothing out with us except small, clear plastic handbags; and we had to exit and enter by one door only. We walked through a metal detector, and a swiveling camera followed us through the door to the parking lot.

I turned in my keys. The metal detector remained silent as I passed through, so the elderly guard at the desk reached for my handbag, examined it, and handed it back, nodding me through.

I thought about what Tina had said about unresolved conflicts and what Dad had said about going for what I wanted and not accepting anything less. The symphony orchestra was too far out of reach, but the tall, handsome guy? Maybe Dad was right. I could give it a try. Why not?

The employee exit was near the outside kitchen door and the huge trash containers. There was a car parked next to the containers. The driver's door was open, and the inside light was on. As I approached, something my size leapt up from the dark plastic bags of trash and squeaked in fright.

Fortunately I recognized one of the assistant chefs in the main kitchen, and just as fortunately, he recognized me. His face had a kind of yellow color, and it wasn't from the car lights. "You scared me to death!" he mumbled.

"What were you doing in the trash bags?" I asked.

"Emptying my ashtray!" he snapped. "I didn't know I had to get your permission!"

Without waiting for me to answer he whirled and leapt into his car, and drove off with a squeal of tires. Apparently I wasn't the only employee who was ready to chew fingernails, but I couldn't understand why I had frightened him so badly.

The roofs of the cars, row after row in the hotel parking lot, gleamed a weird green-blue under powerful arc lamps. I had parked as close to the hotel as I could, but the car Dad had lent me, Old Junk Bucket, was off to one side, the fifth row back. I looked around nervously. I was the only one in the parking lot.

I tucked my car and house keys between the fingers on my right hand, so that they faced outward like small daggers, and made a fist. Tina had shown me how to do this. "Self-preservation is our basic instinct," Tina had said. "If some bozo wants to give you trouble, this will change his mind."

I began walking briskly toward Old Junk Bucket, but soon broke into a run. As I got to the car I was embarrassed to realize that I was making that darned fish noise again. I dropped my keys, scooped them up, and tried to find the one that would open the car door.

I dropped them again.

Where were they? I squatted to find and retrieve them. But my fingers were shaking so much, it was hard to pick up the keys. I tried that relaxing thing again, squeezing my eyes shut and taking two deep breaths. Then slowly I said, "Mary Elizabeth Rafferty, there is nothing to be afraid of."

I opened my eyes and found I was staring at a pair of dark trousers and shoes with somebody in them.

I screamed.

2

Somewhere, high above the shoes, someone yelled, "Don't do that!" and the shoes jumped back.

I shot to my feet, slamming against the side of the car, and stared down at a guy who seemed to be as scared as I was.

He was small-boned, with light-brown hair that stuck up in a cowlick, making a point at the top of his head. He had a pug nose and a narrow chin and looked something like I had imagined Puck ought to look when I read Shakespeare's *Midsummer Night's Dream.*

"What are you doing here?" I screeched at him.

"Room service."

"In the parking lot? You're crazy!"

"Hey, I'm just telling you what I'm doing here. I work in room service. I was on my way home and saw you drop your keys and thought I could help."

I leaned against the side of the car and tried to calm down. "I'm sorry I yelled at you. I was scared."

He looked around, then back at me. "Those arc lamps make the lot bright enough. There's nothing to be scared of."

"I know," I said. "It's just that a few minutes ago somebody came up from the bottom of the pool and grabbed my foot."

He gave me kind of a strange look. "Yeah? Well, I suppose that could scare some people, although I've done that in swimming pools—when I was younger."

I shook my head. "You don't understand. Everybody had gone home, and the pool was dark, and he sneaked in somehow. Oh—forget it."

"You're very pretty," he suddenly said.

It took me by surprise. I dropped my keys again.

He picked them up. "You're really unstrung, aren't you? If you'll wait until I get in my car, I'll follow you home."

"I don't even know you," I said.

"I was going to tell you my name, but when you screamed at me I forgot to."

"I didn't scream! Well, it wasn't a real scream."

"Francis Liverpool III."

"What?"

"That's my given name. *Given,* meaning I didn't choose it. Call me Fran."

"Okay. I'm—"

"I know who you are," Fran said. "We're in the same class at Memorial High."

"We are? But—"

"I know. Because I'm short you think I'm younger than you are. Right? Well, I'm not. I didn't choose being short either."

"I didn't—"

"I don't think lack of height is necessarily genetic. I've got two younger brothers who are going to be tall. One of them is taller than I am already. I think shortness of stature is a direct result of stress. As a matter of fact, someday I'm going to be a geneticist and prove that stress in the classroom inhibits growth."

"Stress in the classroom? But everybody has—"

"Some people more than others. That's going to be part of my study. Does it affect the sincerely conscientious and the creative more than the others? For example, look at football players."

"You keep interrupting me," I said.

Fran looked surprised. "Oh? Sorry. What did you want to say?"

I thought a moment. "Uh—nothing, I guess." *Great conversationalist, Mary Elizabeth Rafferty,* I told myself. I was glad that Fran couldn't see my cheeks turn red.

"Then why don't we go home?" he said. "Remember. I'll follow you."

"I don't need—"

"Yes, you do." Fran turned and walked away.

I drove home with the headlights of Fran's car shining in my rearview mirror. As I pulled into the driveway of our house, he paused, gave a wave, then drove away. Even though Fran drove something that made Old Junk Bucket look good, it had been comforting to have his company on the way home.

I had left a light on in the house. It felt a little funny to be at home alone, but everything in the house was so comfortably familiar I could handle it.

Dad had been sent to Dallas on company business, and Mom had gone with him.

"Are you sure you won't mind being alone?" Mom had asked. "We've never left you alone before. Of course, Mrs. Zellendorf next door has promised to keep an eye on you—uh, on the house."

"Don't talk baby-sitters. I'm a big girl now." I grinned at Mom.

"You could come with us," she suggested.

"No," I said. "I took a job. Remember? Responsibility and all that stuff? Anyhow, I'm going to like the job, and I want to stick with it."

"Good for you," Mom had said as she hugged me, but I had to remind her at least forty times before they drove to the airport that I was going to be all right during the week they'd be gone.

Now I sleepily gave the house a check-over and washed down two of Mom's double-chocolate-chip cookies with a glass of milk. I debated about writing another letter to my best and shortest friend, Amy Peters, who was spending the summer with her father in Connecticut. But I was too tired, so I went to bed. I had time only to smile at the bejeweled audience in Jones Hall and raise my baton before I fell asleep.

Art Mart was working out with the weights when I arrived at the health club the next afternoon. His name is really Arthur Martin, director of the health club and my boss.

"I have to talk to you," I said.

He put down the barbell and flexed his muscles, smiling smugly at his deeply tanned reflection in the huge mirror across the room. Tina told me that Art is the one who had the mirror put in.

"Art," I went on, "I have to tell you what happened last night."

He managed to pull his gaze away from the mirror and turned his attention to me. I was reminded of the facial exercises we had to do in junior-high drama class. First he stared, trying to remember who I was. Then he smiled. And finally, as what I said dawned on him, he scowled. "What happened? You didn't disturb any of the hotel guests, did you?"

"Of course not," I said, and told him about the late-night swimmer.

Art sighed, hitched up his shorts, and started for the outdoor section of the pool. "Come on," he said. "We'll take a look."

I followed him, but not as closely as the appreciative stares of two girls who were splashing around in the shallow water of the indoor pool. They were welcome to him. Art wasn't my type.

"If you think that Art is nothing but a pretty face," Tina had told me during my first day on the job, "you're right."

Mrs. Bandini, one of the afternoon regulars, yoo-hooed at me from her chair across the pool. I just waved back and managed to bang into the edge of the glass door as it swung shut.

I rubbed my shoulder and hurried to catch up with Art. Some little boy was cannonballing into the pool, drenching the sunbathers, who yelled at him.

"It's against the rules," I said to the boy, but he made a face at me and leapt into the water.

I wasn't going to worry about him now. I had to keep up with Art, who dove into a gap in the shrubbery and worked his way along the brick wall, moving toward the left. I thought I'd help, so I did the same thing, working my way toward the right.

Near what should have been a ninety-degree angle in the wall, where a jasmine vine spread itself over the mottled brick, I saw bright cracks of light. I pulled back a handful of vine, startled that it swung so easily, and there it was—a gap at least a foot wide where the two walls didn't meet. The shrubs on both sides of the walls were so thick that the gap was well hidden.

I struggled from the shrubbery, pulling twigs from my hair, and bumped into Art.

"So there you are," he said. "I thought you must have gone back inside to start your shift." He wasn't very subtle. He stared at his watch and then at me.

"I was helping you look," I said.

"It's a waste of time," Art said. "No way anyone could get in or out of here."

"Yes, there is!" I said. "There's a gap where the walls don't meet. I found it!"

He looked surprised. "You're kidding."

"No, I'm not. Go look for yourself."

Art looked at his watch again. "Okay. But you'd better get into the office. And scrub the tiles around the Jacuzzi before you leave tonight. Deeley called in sick this morning, so they didn't get taken care of."

I thought he'd be more excited by my news. "But somebody got into the pool last night. He must have squeezed through that gap."

"Some kid probably," Art said.

"We should have somebody close it."

"I'll get maintenance on it."

"Do you want me to call them when I get to the office?"

"I want you to do your job," he said. "You'll be the only one on duty. I'll take care of it later. G'wan, Liz. Get busy."

Mrs. Bandini waved at me again. Her friend, Mrs. Larabee, had joined her. She waved too. "I've got something to tell you," Mrs. Bandini called.

"I'll be there in a minute," I called back.

Quickly I locked my handbag in the bottom desk

drawer and checked the women's dressing room, picking up a few towels that had been dropped on a bench under the sign saying, PLEASE PUT TOWELS IN THE BASKET. I turned off a shower that had been left dripping and gave the rest room a once-over. I put a fresh stack of towels on the little table next to the door leading from the office to the exercise room, and scanned the pool area from the office window. There seemed to be only four hotel guests and eight club members. It was always pretty quiet in midafternoon. The hotel guests began to arrive around five-thirty. Their business meetings were over, and they were ready for a swim. The club could get pretty crowded during weekday evenings. Even though Art Mart had undoubtedly done the cross-check with the photo-ID cards, I went over them too.

The photo-ID cards were Lamar's idea. As the hotel guests registered at the front desk, they were also automatically registered on film by hidden cameras. They didn't know they were being photographed, and Lamar thought it was better that way. No nonsense about posing or wanting a copy or getting embarrassed because it was a bad shot. He wasn't looking for star quality, Lamar had said. He was simply taking one more step to guard the safety and well-being of all guests of the Ridley Hotel.

The security force studied those photographs, and believe me, there were no strangers wandering around the Ridley Hotel. Duplicate cards were sent each morning and afternoon to the health club along with a list of guests who had checked out, so their cards could be tossed. The cards of regular club members, who lived in Houston, were also on file.

I liked to go over the cards. It helped me to remember names, and everyone likes to be addressed by name.

It was also fun to study the types of faces and wonder who each person was and what he or she was like. There were glum faces and eager faces and faces with expressions from peevish to placid. Opening the card file and thumbing through it, guessing about the people behind the faces, made me think of opening a box of smooth-looking chocolates and trying to figure out which hid the chocolate creams and which held the cherries. Some of the faces stayed a few days and became familiar. Some came and disappeared and came back again. Some popped in on an afternoon, but were on their way the next day and never returned.

I glanced at Sylvia Bandini's card. She was a club member, here every day. Tina said that Mrs. Bandini had celebrated her seventieth birthday last May. Mrs. Bandini's white hair curled around her face like the frame around a portrait. She read all the latest exercise books and tried to look like the models on the book jackets. Once she even wore striped red-and-green leg warmers with her blue bathing suit. On a scale of one to ten she would have got a ten for trying, but her figure was kind of a minus five. She was really nice. Her smile was always a bright-red gleam across the room, and I liked to talk to her.

Her friend, Mrs. Opal Larabee, was five years younger than Mrs. Bandini. Mrs. Larabee pointedly mentioned this soon after I met the two women. Mrs. Bandini just smiled and added that Mrs. Larabee was one up on her there, and was also one up on her where weight was concerned, being fifteen pounds heavier. Mrs. Larabee smiled and said something about being an inch and three quarters taller, and I left in a hurry, not wanting to hear the rest.

Mr. Asmir Kamara was at the club, as usual. I twisted to

glance through the wide glass window wall that divided the office from the pool area and saw his shining bald head leading the way back and forth in a straight path from one end of the pool to the other. His daily routine. As usual, his terry-cloth robe was folded neatly over the back of a chair, and his thongs were placed side by side under the chair. Mr. Kamara, a wealthy retiree who lived at the Ridley Hotel, seemed to speak only enough English to imperiously insult all the male employees of the hotel and extravagantly flatter all the female employees.

"Watch out for that old buzzard," Tina had told me. "In his country they have some funny ideas about women. If he pesters you, give me a call and I'll come running."

Art Mart was more blunt. "He'll probably ask you to go away with him for a weekend. So far he's tried it with all the women who work in the hotel. When you turn him down, remember he's a guest of the Ridley and go easy."

Mr. Kamara introduced himself to me on my first day at work. The next afternoon, when he arrived at the club, wearing a terry-cloth robe over his bathing trunks, he brought me a bunch of blue-dyed carnations and a bag of apples. "You will drive to New Orleans with me this weekend?" he asked.

I tried to remember the clever retort I had planned to answer, but all that came out was "No."

He just shrugged. "Maybe later."

"No," I said.

He seemed to hesitate, then shoved the flowers and bag of apples at me. "Keep anyway," he said, and flashed an expensive porcelain smile.

"No, thanks," I said.

"Yes, thanks," he said firmly, put them on my desk, and disappeared into the men's dressing room to lock his room key and wallet in his locker. He returned in a few minutes, going straight through the office to his favorite, somewhat secluded, table and chair, where he was joined by a club member named C. L. Jones.

Mr. Jones, who was pale and long and skinny, had what my PE teacher called sloppy posture. His shoulders were so rounded he looked like the top of a question mark. He was as unusual as Mr. Kamara. Tina told me that Mr. Jones came every day to the club, but he rarely went swimming and never stayed very long. Sometimes he rode the exercise bike, but mostly he chatted awhile with Mr. Kamara and left. His membership seemed like a waste of money.

Mrs. Bandini's arms rippled up and down in some kind of a signal to me, so I put the box of photo-ID cards back in the desk, left the office, and walked over to where she and Mrs. Larabee were ensconced in their deck chairs with cups of coffee.

"Such a nice girl," Mrs. Bandini said, and gleamed at me. "I would like to have a granddaughter like you, Mary Elizabeth."

"You would like to have a granddaughter, period," Mrs. Larabee said, "although there's small chance of that."

Mrs. Bandini looked pained. "I have two grandsons, who are a constant joy, as you well know, and if my daughter, Rosa, wanted to go to law school instead of becoming mother to a beautiful little daughter, who was I to tell her what a mistake she was making?"

My legs were suddenly splattered with cold water, and I jumped back. Climbing out of the pool was the boy who'd been cannonballing. "Listen, you—" I began.

But Mrs. Bandini interrupted me. "Mary Elizabeth, I'd like you to meet my youngest grandson, Paul Canelli.

He's ten years old and getting straight A's in school, and you should hear him play the piano. Pauly's teacher says he has exceptional talent. Shake hands with Mary Elizabeth, Pauly."

She was so proud of him I ignored Pauly's smirk. I held out my hand, hoping he wouldn't bite it.

He shook my hand as quickly as possible, grabbed a towel, and wrapped it around himself. He flopped into a chair and said, "Could I have a hamburger, Grandma?"

"You'll spoil your dinner," Mrs. Bandini said.

"But I'm hungry. Please, Grandma?"

"Well . . ." Mrs. Bandini hesitated only a second. "If you promise to eat all your dinner tonight, you may phone for room service."

Room service. I thought about Fran. He was a funny little guy, but I hoped I'd see him again today. Maybe I should look him up. I'd like to thank him for escorting me home last night. I'd like him to see that I wasn't always as weird as I must have seemed last night.

Pauly ran over to the phone. Mr. Kamara was just putting the receiver on its hook. Pauly ducked in to grab it, and Mr. Kamara nearly fell over him. He caught his balance and snapped something at Pauly in a language I didn't understand. It was probably just as well.

Mrs. Bandini was speaking to me, so I made myself pay attention.

". . . my other grandson, Eric," she said. "All the girls like Eric. He's very handsome. Very tall too. I told him about you, Mary Elizabeth."

She stopped and seemed to be waiting for an answer. I stammered the first thing that came to mind. "He must be wonderful."

"Oh, he is," she said. "I'm going to make sure that the two of you meet each other."

"Great," I said, trying to sound enthusiastic. The last thing I wanted to do was meet Mrs. Bandini's other grandson. One was more than enough.

I went toward the office as Floyd Parmlee came into the room with a covered tray. I had met Floyd on Monday. He was as bland on the inside as he was on the outside. He reminded me of yellow wax beans. I hate yellow wax beans.

Mr. Kamara had picked a table off to the side, behind a large potted plant, where he couldn't be seen by the people at the pool. But as I neared the office door I saw Floyd put the tray on the table next to Mr. Kamara, who signed for whatever it was he ordered. Then I saw something strange. It took only a second, but through the fronds of the potted plant I know I saw Mr. Kamara shove some money into Floyd's hand. It looked like a lot of money. Wow! Talk about big tippers!

I was seated at the desk, getting ready to start writing my daily report, when Floyd poked his head in the door. He shoved a gold-foil-covered box at me.

"What's that?" I asked.

"From Mr. Kamara," Floyd said. "It's chocolates from the gift shop."

"I don't want them."

"Why not?"

"Because I can't accept them. I can't have Mr. Kamara giving me presents. Will you tell him that, Floyd?"

"Tell him yourself," Floyd said. "It's no skin off my nose." He disappeared.

I picked up the box of chocolates as though it were a bomb and carried it out to where Mr. Kamara was sitting, eating a dish of strawberry ice cream.

"I'm sorry, Mr. Kamara," I said, knowing that Mrs. Bandini and Mrs. Larabee were as intent on what I was saying as Mr. Kamara was, "but I can't accept your presents."

"Yes," Mr. Kamara said. His broad smile was decorated with a strand of crushed strawberry. "I want you to take."

"I can't take. I mean, it's not proper for an employee to accept gifts from a hotel guest."

"I not understand," Mr. Kamara said. "Is chocolates. Girls like chocolates. You eat."

"No, thank you," I said firmly, placing the box in front of him.

"Yes, thank you," he said, just as firmly.

From the corner of my eye I saw Fran enter the room with a tray and make a beeline to where Pauly was sitting.

I stood as tall as I could and tried to intimidate Mr. Kamara. "You must stop giving me gifts, Mr. Kamara."

"Yes," he said. "No more. But you take now." He handed the box of chocolates to me again. As I hesitated he repeated, "No more."

Without a word, mainly because I couldn't think of the right thing to say, I took the box and marched back to the office.

In a few minutes Fran appeared. "Hi," he said.

"Hi. I'm glad you're here."

His eyes seemed to spark. "You are? Really?"

"Yes. Thanks for escorting me home last night."

"Yeah. Well, sure." He looked pleased with himself. "Now I know where you live, maybe I could come by sometime, if it's all right with you."

Four inches shorter than I am, and asking me for a date? How could I go out with a guy who'd make me look even taller than I am? Besides, I had a goal to work on. Tall and handsome. Keep the thought in mind. "Uh— I'm—uh—kind of busy right now," I said.

Fran just shrugged. He glanced at a slip of paper in his hand. "Those women over there—Mrs. Bandini and Mrs. Larabee. They said if you didn't want to eat the chocolates, if you were worried that chocolate might cause skin problems in teenagers, they'd help you out."

"In other words they wish I'd give them the box of chocolates."

"Mrs. Bandini said to tell you that box sells for twenty-four dollars and ninety-eight cents in the gift shop."

I giggled, and Fran laughed too.

"What should I do about Mr. Kamara?" I asked. "He's, uh—unusual."

"Weird," Fran said. "Floyd usually gets him and complains about it."

"What do you mean?"

"Mr. Kamara's order. He always wants Floyd to deliver it, and Floyd grumbles about it a lot, because he says Mr. Kamara hardly ever tips, and then it's only a quarter or fifty cents, no matter how much the order is."

"But—" I said.

Fran went on. "He's a real tightwad and crabby to everyone and . . ."

I stopped listening. I was thinking about the fistful of bills I had seen Mr. Kamara hand to Floyd. Something about that transaction was decidedly strange.

3

Fran finally ran down, and I said, "Listen to me. A few minutes ago I saw Mr. Kamara hand Floyd what looked like a fistful of bills."

"Maybe to buy the candy for you." Fran glanced down at the gold-foil box.

"There's one way to find out." I rang the gift shop and Mrs. Landon answered. We had the same shift, and we'd eaten dinner together in the employee cafeteria two days in a row. I was sure she'd answer my question, and she did.

I thanked her, hung up, and said to Fran, "He charged it to his room. He charges everything to his room."

"So?" Fran asked. "There are lots of reasons he could be giving Floyd money. Like maybe Floyd asked for a loan."

"Maybe," I said. "It just didn't seem right. And there are so many strange things going on that I—Never mind. It's really not my business what Mr. Kamara does. I suppose I'm poking my nose where it doesn't belong."

"It's a good-looking nose. Take care of it," Fran said. He smiled and left the office.

He was a nice guy with a kind of relaxed friendliness that made him easy to talk to. But four inches shorter? Forget it.

I took the box of candy to Mrs. Bandini, staying only long enough to watch Pauly dive into it with both hands. Mr. Kamara was in the pool again, swimming back and forth. He opened one eye and rolled it until it focused on me. He reminded me of a film I'd seen on whales, and I wouldn't have been surprised if he'd suddenly spouted water. He scowled at the box of chocolates, dived underwater with a snort, and returned to his rhythmic pattern, ignoring us.

"My grandson, Eric, is even taller than you are and very handsome," Mrs. Bandini said. "You'd like him. The girls he knows—always telephoning him, always chasing him. He needs to meet a nice girl like you."

I wondered if he shoveled chocolates into his face as fast as Pauly did. "I've got to get back to work," I told her, and hurried to the office. A deep canvas cart, which was piled to the top with freshly laundered towels, had been brought down; and I had to stack them in the office closet.

A towel cart came down twice a day—in the morning before the club opened, and in the middle of the afternoon. Art Mart took care of the towels in the morning, even before the club opened and Deeley arrived. Deeley Johnson, who worked in the health club on the morning shift, said that Art was really fussy about having the fresh towels stacked before the first swimmer arrived.

The rest of the afternoon and evening were busier than usual. A convention group registered, and many of their members seemed to head for the pool and Jacuzzi as soon as they had checked in. Tina brought in a batch of photo-ID cards, and I studied them carefully, doing my best to tie faces to names.

Tina, who had stayed and was staring out the office window toward the inside section of the pool, nudged my shoulder. "Who's the hunk over there with the red hair? Look him up. Quick."

"He's married and has eight children," I said.

Tina whirled and blinked at me a couple of times before she met my answering grin. "I knew that stuff wasn't on the card," she said. "Come on. What's his name?"

I pulled the card and told her.

"See you later," she said, and sauntered around the pool in the guy's direction.

Deeley called in to report that she'd be out sick again the next day. Deeley was always ready to leave as I arrived, so besides comparing notes on our jobs and some of the people who came to the club, we hadn't had much chance to talk. I told her that I hoped she'd be well soon and went back to work.

Finally, as the crowd began thinning, Art Mart returned to the club. He sat at the desk, humming to himself, then seemed to notice me. "How about the tiles, Liz? It's a good time to clean them. There's no one in the Jacuzzi right now."

"Okay," I said. I pulled the brush I needed from the closet. Art had tilted back his chair and propped his feet on the desk. "Will you be here until closing time?" As I asked the question I knew it came out sounding desperate.

Art didn't notice. Maybe it was all that carefully combed thick blond hair that kept subtleties from penetrating his mind. Something certainly got in the way. "Naw," Art drawled. "I got a date."

I shifted the brush from one hand to the other and back again. "What did maintenance say?"

"About what?"

"About the gap between the walls?"

Art mulled this over for a moment, then said, "Guess I forgot to tell them about it."

"But what if whoever sneaked in last night comes back?"

He grinned. "He won't. From what you told me, you probably scared him worse than he scared you."

"Why don't you call maintenance right now?"

"Won't do any good. Nobody's there at night."

"Somebody's always there."

"Nobody but one night-man on duty in case a pipe breaks or something. I'll call in the morning."

"You won't forget?"

He just stared at me with a disgusted look. "Don't rub it in. Didn't you ever forget something?"

"Oh," I said. "I almost forgot to tell you that Deeley won't be back tomorrow morning. She's still sick."

He let out an obscenity and grumbled something about not wanting to get up that early. But his mood suddenly changed, and he leaned across the desk to point a finger at me. "Ha! You almost forgot to tell me! Don't get after me ever again for forgetting something!"

"I won't," I said, and scooted out of the office.

Scrubbing tiles is hard work, but I did a good, thorough job of it. Now and then someone would call out a friendly good-bye to me, and I'd sit back on my heels and chat a moment before getting back to work. But when I finally stood, mission accomplished, I found it was five minutes to closing time, and I was the only one in the health club.

The swimming pool was bright and gleaming with

light, and it was going to stay that way until the moment I left this place. My steps quickened, and I went through the routine of tidying both locker rooms and checking to make sure no one was left in the rest rooms or saunas. With everything taken care of I unlocked the bottom desk drawer and retrieved my handbag.

Clutching it and the health-club keys tightly, I flipped off all the lights as fast as I could, locked the office door, and sprinted toward the door that connected the health club with the hotel.

So much for plans. In the darkness I slammed into a body that made an oofing sound and wrapped its arms tightly around me. Down we dropped, legs thrashing. I fell on top of whoever it was, and he let out a yell.

"I have a weapon," I said fiercely, wondering where my handbag and key ring had landed. "Don't move, or you're dead."

"I hope *you* move. You're squashing me," he grunted.

I recognized his voice. "Fran? What are you doing there?"

"You knocked me down." His words came out in gasps. "Get up, Liz! You're heavy, and your elbow is in my stomach!"

I quickly rolled away and sat up. Fran sat up too. My eyes were becoming accustomed to the darkness, so I could see Fran rubbing the back of his head.

"I'm sorry," I said. "I didn't know you were in the club."

"I thought I'd help you close up," he said. "I guessed that you were still a little jumpy."

I was really touched. "Fran," I said, "what a nice, kind thing to do."

He reached for my hand and held it. His hand was warm and strong. "What kind of a weapon?" he asked.

"What are you talking about?"

"You said you had a weapon. You said if I moved you'd kill me."

"Oh," I said. "The health-club keys, but I dropped them along with my handbag."

"How do you key somebody to death?" Fran asked. He put an arm around my shoulders and moved closer.

"Don't be so literal."

"Don't make threats you can't carry out." Without a pause he added, "Very interesting. Your height is in your legs."

"What?"

"You have very long legs," he said, "which look good in shorts. I noticed. But all legs aside, the point I'm trying to make is that when we're sitting down our bodies are the same height. See?"

"Oh," I said, "you're right."

"So maybe we could meet in a café—something elegant, like Flakey Jake's or Showtime Pizza."

"Those aren't elegant. They're fast-food restaurants."

"Look, I don't have all the money in the world. You'll have to restrain your greedy impulses."

"My what?"

"Pay attention. You can be seated, looking lonely and romantic, and I'll come in and sit across from you and take your hand."

"Come on, Fran—"

"I'm trying to."

"Listen—"

He just smiled. "See how it works? We can both be sitting down the whole time, and relative heights won't matter."

"What about when we leave?"

"One of us will just have to leave before the other one."

"It will be me," I said. "I'll arise, still looking lonely and romantic, and drift out of your life."

"We're losing something here," he said. "Let me think of another example."

I heard the whirr of the camera in the corner as it swept the room. In a few seconds the telephone in the office began to ring.

"I know just who that is," I said, and ran toward the office, turning on the light. I was right.

"What happened to you, Liz?" Tina asked. "I knew you were scared, so I kept you on camera. You turned off the lights, but you didn't leave the room. Are you still testing your subconscious mind's resistance to the dark?"

"Something like that," I said.

"Well, after this, warn me," she said. "I got worried about you, and I couldn't leave the camera, because Lamar's on duty checking the bar."

"I'm sorry," I said.

"You were right," she said. "He's married."

"Lamar?"

"No, the guy with red hair. There was another cute one, though. Broad shoulders, brown hair. If he's still here tomorrow I'll take a look at his card."

Tina hung up.

"Let's go," I said to Fran.

We locked up and headed for the employee check-out. Lamar was there, chatting with his assistant at the desk. He was leaning casually against the wall, although he managed to give the impression of being ready to spring into action. I don't know how he did it. Maybe it was the way he made his eyes into slits and looked at us down the end of his nose.

"We may soon have to insist on body searches," Lamar said.

"I think that would be illegal," Fran told him.

"Illegal!" Lamar straightened and glared down at Fran. "We're talking about major theft, and you're bringing up trivia."

"But there are laws protecting human rights."

Lamar sighed. "Human? With the amount of stuff being snatched out of this hotel, it couldn't be done by any human."

"Hmmm," Fran said. "Trained dogs?"

Lamar gave Fran a withering look that would have made Clint Eastwood jealous. "This is serious business," he said. "Yesterday someone made it out of here with an antique silver tray, a Waterford vase from the presidential suite, fourteen boxes of Brie cheese, and five standing rib roasts. This is the only employee exit to the hotel. Now you tell me how the thief managed it."

"Maybe he threw everything out of a window," Fran said.

"A Waterford vase?" Lamar sneered. "Besides, the hotel is designed for air-conditioning. None of the windows open."

"Then maybe he just walked out the front door."

"No way. One of my assistants is at the front door at all times."

Fran rubbed his chin and his eyes began to gleam. I could tell he was enjoying matching his wits against the thief's. "Maybe the guests are stealing the things you talked about."

"Guests do a lot of stealing, that's true," Lamar said, "but we can tell when the thief is a guest and when it's an employee, because guests will steal from their own rooms or restaurant tables. Employees steal from places the guests don't go."

"Suppose the thief disguised himself, dressed like a guest, and walked out with a suitcase full of stuff."

"It wouldn't work," Lamar said. "Remember our photo-ID cards? We'd spot anyone who didn't match one of the cards."

"Okay, then," Fran said. "This guy's got an accomplice. They meet in the bar, and he passes the stuff to him. Or maybe it's a her."

"Nope," Lamar said. "My scrutinizing system's too good to let that one go by."

Fran thought so hard his forehead wrinkled. Finally he said, "Let me work on it. I'll come up with something."

"Sure you will," Lamar said. "You ready to check out of here?"

"Yes." I stepped forward. Lamar carefully examined my plastic handbag, although it was obvious there was nothing in it but a very thin wallet, a lipstick, a comb, and my car keys. I walked through the metal detector, which remained silent. It wouldn't be possible to sneak anything out under my pink health-club T-shirt and shorts, but Lamar scowled at me as though I'd managed to pull a fast one.

Fran sauntered through, and again the detector was silent, so we said good-night to Lamar and left the hotel.

"The evening is early," Fran said as we walked toward my car. "Want to meet somewhere for a Coke?"

"Fran, it's eleven-thirty. That is not early."

"It's all in the point of view," Fran said. "Besides, how can we go home and sleep, knowing that while we are secure in our beds a thief is robbing the Ridley Hotel and sneaking out through a secret exit unknown to our vigilant chief of security?"

Secret exit? I abruptly stopped, gasped, and clutched Fran's arm.

"What? Where? What's the matter?" His head twisted from side to side as he tried to take in the entire parking lot.

"I didn't *see* anything. I *thought* of something."

"Don't think so violently. Think gently. When you bugged out your eyes and made a kind of fish noise, you scared me. I thought something was creeping up on us."

"Stop trying to be funny and listen to me," I said. "There *is* a secret exit from the hotel. Remember when I told you that somebody in the pool had sneaked in, and it scared me? Well, I found the way he got in. There's a one-foot gap where two walls don't meet, but they're covered with vines, so the gap can't be seen."

Fran's eyes widened. "Show me."

"Let's tell Lamar first. I can show both of you."

We walked back to the employee entrance. Lamar was still there, talking to the guard behind the desk. In a rush of words I told Lamar about the wall.

For a few moments he contemplated what I had said, and as he thought he became even more of a tall, straight line. "We'll check it out," he told us, "although I'm looking at one flaw and one distinct impossibility."

"You're talking about Liz and me. Right?" Fran asked.

Lamar stared down his nose at Fran as though he were something he'd found on his shoe. "Come with me," he answered. "We'll take a look."

He picked up the health-club keys and a flashlight from the desk and strode briskly down the hall, across the side lobby, and into the hall leading to the health club. Fran and I trotted after him, trying to keep up.

First, Lamar tried the door, but it was locked, just as I had left it. He opened it and went inside. Fran and I were right on his heels. Literally. Because it was dark, Lamar suddenly stopped and we smashed into him.

"Ouch!" he said. "Where's the light switch?"

"They didn't put it near the door," I said. "The switches are all inside the office."

By this time our eyes were becoming adjusted to the darkness. It helped that a large moon had turned the outside section of the pool into a frosted mirror. We could see the shapes of the tables and chairs and each other. The limbs and leaves of the large potted plants and trees jutted out in every direction, as though they were doing a crazy dance. I moved a little closer to Fran and took his hand.

Lamar gave a couple of hops as he pulled up the back of his left shoe, which I had unfortunately stepped on. He strode to the door of the health-club office, tried the door, then fiddled with the keys until he found the one that unlocked it, while I stared into the glimmering black water of the indoor section of the pool and the puddled tiles near my feet. I got that peculiar, uncomfortable feeling that something was wrong; but what it was I didn't know.

The office door swung open, and in an instant the indoor and outdoor lights flashed on. There was no one in the pool. Of course there wouldn't be.

"Where's this gap in the walls?" Lamar asked.

We pushed open the door in the glass divider wall to get outside, propping it open so it wouldn't close and lock us out. We circled the far end of the pool. With his flashlight Lamar led the way, following my directions. He pulled back the vines and swept his light over the wall and the surrounding area. He focused on the spongy humus-earth mixture near the wall.

"Plenty of footprints," he said. "This soft earth is good for prints."

"Some of them might be mine," I told him.

"Yep," he answered. "Those narrow size nine with the herringbone imprint. Let's see the bottom of your tennis shoes."

I wished he hadn't been so explicit. I held up one foot and he nodded.

"Okay," he said. "Let's go back inside, and I'll go over my findings."

"What findings?" Fran asked. "All we came up with was a gap between two walls, and not a very big one at that."

"Big enough for someone to squeeze through," I said.

"Art Mart was probably right. It must have been a kid," Fran said.

Lamar didn't answer. He just strode back to the inside section of the health club, looking as controlled as ever. Even struggling through the shrubbery hadn't put a wrinkle in his suit, although I had to pull a few more leaves out of my hair and tug my T-shirt back into place.

He locked the glass door and turned to us. "All right. This is what we found. Although there were no complete footprints, we could see a number of fresh partial ones. Between the walls were adult-sized shoeprints heading toward the pool, and part of a bare footprint on top of one of them heading out, which tells us that someone had entered wearing shoes, but had taken them off before returning."

"Oh!" I interrupted. "He took off his shoes and dived into the pool. That's when we saw each other. So he swam back and got out of there in a hurry, not waiting to put his shoes back on again."

"And it wasn't a kid," Fran said.

"That's right," Lamar told him.

Fran rubbed his hands together. I could tell he was getting excited. "There were a number of prints, so we can tell that the guy's been here before. He sneaks in, robs the hotel, then sneaks out with the stuff the same way."

"Wrong," Lamar said. "He could get into the pool area, but there's no way he could get from there into the main part of the hotel."

"The door would be locked," I told him. "And, for that matter, so would the door into the health-club office."

"The office door could be jimmied," Lamar said, "which is the flaw I spoke of. The door into the hotel, however, has a dead-bolt type of lock, and it couldn't be opened without a key. That's the impossibility I mentioned."

"You're very clever." I was really impressed.

Lamar's eyes narrowed and his upper lip curled modestly. Clint Eastwood would have loved this expression. "It's my job," Lamar said.

He walked into the office, turned out all the lights, and locked the office door.

"Wait a minute," Fran said. "What does all this mean?"

"That somebody just wanted a swim," Lamar said.

"Could there be something in the office this guy was after?"

"There's nothing valuable in there," I told him, "except the equipment. It's heavy, and it's too big to get through anything but a full-sized door."

"Forget it," Lamar said. "And put a move on. I've got other things to do here, and your parents are going to start wondering why you didn't get home on time."

He locked the main door behind us and handed me the keys. "Turn these in when you leave. I've got to do another bar check."

Lamar strode off, but I turned to Fran. "Something's bothering me."

"Probably your conscience. Have you changed your mind about meeting me for a Coke?"

"Be serious, and be quiet. I'm trying to think." I spoke aloud. "The pool, the pool. The water in the pool. The puddles on the tiles." I stared at Fran. "That's it! The water on the tiles! It shouldn't have been there!"

"Go on," Fran said, and I was glad that he was paying attention and not trying to be funny.

"What I'm saying is that my last job is to put the club in order. I put away used towels, throw out the used soap in the showers, toss away paper cups and napkins and rubbish people leave around, and do a last-minute inspection around the pool. Usually there aren't many people at the pool during the last hour, and the puddles on the tiles drain and dry fast. By the time I leave, those tiles don't even have wet footprints on them. And I could swear there were no puddles on the tiles when I locked up tonight. But when we went back there with Lamar I noticed water on the tiles near where we were standing."

"Can we go back and look again?"

I nodded. "Let's hurry."

We unlocked the door to the pool area. Once inside the room we kept our backs to the door, breathing in the smell of warm chlorine and jungle dampness until our eyes became accustomed to the darkness.

"No one's here now," Fran whispered. "That is, I can't see anyone except us."

As fast as possible I scurried to the office door, fumbled the keys, and finally got it open. I stepped inside and turned on the lights.

Fran was standing outside the office door staring at a spot on the tiles around the pool. "Right over there," he said, and pointed.

"Yes. Someone used the pool to sneak in here." I looked at the puddle of water that dripped across the tiles. Automatically Fran and I moved forward, following it.

It stopped abruptly in front of one of the large potted ficus trees.

"What happened to him?" Fran murmured. "He couldn't just dissolve. He had to go somewhere."

I held my breath as I slowly looked upward into the slender branches over our heads.

4

No one was there.

If someone had been looking back at me, I think I would have fainted or screamed or maybe fallen in the pool and drowned, I was that frightened.

Fran wasn't any braver. As he felt around the top of the big brass planter, I could see his fingers tremble. "Funny," he said. His voice cracked and he started over, speaking a little more slowly and a little deeper. "It's funny, but it's damp right here and around the trunk of the tree in this one spot."

I put my hand where he showed me. "It's like someone took hold of the trunk of the tree."

Fran let out a long sigh. "Maybe we've come across some kind of a relay tag race that involves diving into the pool, climbing out, touching the tree, diving in again, and—oh, well. It's an idea."

"Not a very good one."

"Have you got a better one?"

The telephone in the office rang, and I jumped straight up in the air.

I ran to answer, and it was Tina. "Your mother called

from Dallas, and because the club is officially closed the switchboard referred the call to me. She was all excited because you hadn't got home yet. Anyhow, I saw you on camera with Lamar, so I told her you were helping the chief of security on a special project and would be home in half an hour. What are you doing in the health club?"

"Fran and I were investigating a puddle."

"There are better things to do with your spare time. You'd better get on home right away and call your mother."

"I thought you were off duty," I said.

"I will be as soon as Harvey gets here for his shift. He forgot to get his car inspected and had to take a bus."

"Thanks for covering for me, Tina," I said. "See you tomorrow."

I turned off the lights and locked the office door. Fran and I left the club and the hotel and the parking lot, the latter only after I convinced Fran I didn't want to go somewhere for a Coca-Cola.

"Have you ever heard of the theory of relativity?" Fran asked.

"Of course. Einstein. But I don't understand it."

"Very few people do," Fran said. "Sometime I'll explain it to you. It has to do with height."

"No, it doesn't."

"Yes, it does. You said you didn't understand it, and you were right. Basically, when you get past all the equations, it boils down to the fact that if two people like each other, relative heights between them are meaningless."

"Good night, Fran," I said. "I'll see you tomorrow." I couldn't imagine why, but I was looking forward to it.

With gusto and flair I conducted the most dramatic part of Wagner's *Ride of the Valkyries* as I drove home.

As soon as I got inside the house I called Mom at their hotel in Dallas. She was still wide awake.

"I'm fine," I said.

"I just wanted to make sure," Mom said.

"You don't need to worry about me."

"Oh, darling, I wouldn't! Not for a minute!" Mom answered, then began a list of questions, beginning with "Are you eating a nourishing breakfast?" and ending with "Are you sure you're fine? I just had this strange, shivery feeling that everything might not be quite all right."

"Relax, Mom. Things are okay," I said. I didn't tell Mom that I was carrying around a strange, shivery feeling too.

I arrived at the Ridley the next afternoon at the same time as four men dressed in white duck jumpsuits. A fifth man had backed a large van up to the double doors next to the employee entrance. The men followed me into the hotel. I planned to hold out my plastic handbag to be examined, but I dropped it, and as I suddenly stopped to pick it up, one of the men fell over me.

"I'm very sorry," I said, trying to help him up, pick myself up, and get a grip on my handbag at the same time.

"No problem," he grumbled, and glared at me.

He was young and tall and kind of cute. I smiled and started to say something casually friendly. But it's hard to be casually friendly to someone who's rubbing his elbow because it hurts, and it's all your fault, so I let the whole thing drop and held my handbag out to the guard at the desk.

But the man who was carrying a clipboard leaned over

the desk and said to the security guard, "Somebody gotta sign this order form."

"The manager's always out for lunch at this time, so I'll get Mr. Boudry for you," the guard said, and he pressed a couple of buttons.

"Will you please look at my handbag?" I asked the guard.

He took it, and the man with the clipboard looked at it too. "What's so special about it?" he asked me. "I've seen better-looking handbags than that."

"It's a security regulation," I told him.

He shrugged. "You got tight security here?"

"Absolutely," I said.

"The best," the guard said. He handed back my handbag just as Lamar strode in. Lamar ignored me, eagle-eyeing the men in white uniforms. As I left I heard one of them telling Lamar, "We got orders to pick up two ten-foot sofas to be cleaned. Have you got enough authority to sign this?"

I walked on to the health club through the side lobby, glancing into the main lobby as I passed. There were only two ten-foot sofas in the hotel, and they were gorgeous and probably terribly expensive, with hand-carved mahogany framing coral-and-silver brocade. They didn't look as though they needed cleaning to me, but hotel managers must know what they're doing.

Mr. Jones and Mr. Kamara were seated as far from the pool area as they could get, behind a large potted palm tree. Their plastic lounge chairs sagged under their weight as the men leaned close to each other. Mr. Kamara was wearing bathing trunks, but Mr. Jones was dressed in a wrinkled gray suit. He was probably hot, because his face was red, and he kept rubbing at his forehead with a handkerchief. With his other hand he

kept batting away a palm tree frond that dipped low
enough to tickle his head. All that mopping and batting
made him look like a wiggling gray spider.

But Mr. Kamara wasn't the fly. Instead, he looked as
though he could eat Mr. Jones, with or without ketchup. I
couldn't tell what the two men were saying, because the
gurgling, bubbling Jacuzzi drowned out their words, but
each time Mr. Kamara hit his fist on the arm of the
lounge chair, Mr. Jones winced and shuddered.

"Liz!"

I jumped as Art Mart yelled at me from the open office
doorway. "You're five minutes late!"

"Sorry!" It took only seconds to reach the office.

"A large convention of insurance salesmen will be
here for the next three days, and they've already started
coming into the club. So get with it, will you?"

I'd never seen him this grouchy, but I didn't let his
rudeness bother me. What can you expect from someone
like Art? Not much. "I'm with it," I told him. "On duty.
Bright and cheerful."

He actually growled at me, snatched his car keys out of
the desk, and said, "I'm off. Got stuff to do."

"Are you going to be back?"

"Maybe yes, maybe no."

"But you said the club would be really busy."

"So what? I hired you because I thought you could do
the job. How smart do you have to be to pick up dirty
towels? If you don't think you can handle it, just say so."

It would have given me a great deal of pleasure to tell
him what I was thinking about him, but I wanted to hang
on to my job. So I quietly said, "I can handle it."

Without another word he strode out of the office.

I completed my check of the women's dressing room
and sauna, but there were guests in the men's section.

Art was right. The club was getting busy in a hurry. I toured the pool area, stopping to say hello to Mrs. Bandini and Mrs. Larabee, and passed Mr. Jones, who was leaving the club. "Good-bye," I said cheerfully, but he didn't seem to hear me. He pushed through the door, head down, muttering to himself.

Just as I sat at the desk Tina popped into the office. "Hi," she said. "Ready?"

"For what?"

"Card file." She handed me a stack of cards an inch thick. "Here are the new ones, and while you're busy filing them, let's see if we can't find that good-looking guy's card."

"What's his name?"

"I don't know, but he's out there right now, sunning himself. He's already got a great tan."

I pulled the file from the side drawer and handed it to her. "Here. While I study the new ones, you can look through the file and find his name."

While Tina was busy with the file, I checked in four guests, mentally matched their faces to their cards, handed them towels, and smilingly said that I hoped they enjoyed their stay in the Ridley health club.

As I went back to the desk, Tina snapped shut the lid of the file and looked puzzled. "So where is he?"

"Who?"

"The guy with the brown hair. His card isn't in here."

"Maybe he checked out."

"No. I told you. He's out there sunning himself."

"Maybe the card was misfiled."

"I went through the whole thing."

"Do you suppose he's not really a guest here? We could ask security to check."

Tina stood up and smiled. "I'm security. Remember?

And what a good excuse to start a conversation. See you later."

She zipped out the doorway, heading for the outside pool—just as a small body dashed past her and cannonballed into the pool, sending up a sheet of water.

Tina jumped back, glaring and muttering, and snatched up a towel. As she blotted the spots on her uniform she said, "This is your department. Yell at him. Kick him out. Have him arrested for impersonating a human being."

I had seen who it was. Pauly Canelli. "I'll be stern," I said, and marched to the side of the pool. Pauly had surfaced and was grinning at me.

"I told you not to do that," I said.

"I forgot."

"No, you didn't."

"What are you gonna do about it?"

I put my fists on my hips and tried to look tough and mean. "Out of the pool!"

"I'll tell my grandma."

"Out!"

He swam to the shallow end, near to the chair in which his grandmother was enthroned. I walked around the edge of the pool to meet him. I noticed two men in business suits standing by the door to the hotel. Perhaps they were new guests. I should find out, but I had to take care of Pauly first.

Mrs. Bandini was all smiles as Pauly ran to her. She enfolded him in a large beach towel and beamed at me. "Isn't he a lovely boy? Both of my grandchildren are such a joy to me."

"She made me get out of the pool," Pauly whined.

Mrs. Bandini's eyes grew wide. "Why?"

"He was cannonballing people," I said. "I told him not to."

Mrs. Bandini chuckled. "I thought it was something important. Well, Pauly won't do it anymore, will you, Pauly, my love?" Without waiting for his answer she said to him, "Why don't you ring up room service and get something good to eat, like a hamburger and milk shake? And later you can go back in the pool if Liz says you can, and I'm sure she will."

"It's okay," I mumbled, wishing I had handled things better.

As Pauly ran to the house phone, Mrs. Bandini confided, "He's so much like his big brother Eric was at that age. So full of life and fun and mischief."

I just smiled back. What could I say?

"I can't wait until you and Eric meet each other," Mrs. Bandini added.

As far as I was concerned, I hoped that day would never come. I glanced at the door and saw that the two men in business suits were still there. They were both about my height and stocky. They were old enough to have jowls, and the dark-haired one could have used a shampoo. "Excuse me," I said to Mrs. Bandini, and walked toward the guests.

"May I help you?" I asked them.

"No," the greasy-haired one said, but the other nudged him.

"Maybe," he said. "There was a guy who left here a little while ago. Kind of skinny and stooped."

"Wearing a gray suit," the first man added.

They had to mean Mr. Jones, but I didn't see any reason to answer their questions. I didn't know who they were. I just stared at them until Greasy said, "You know who we're talking about?"

"Are you guests of the Ridley Hotel?"

"What's that got to do with anything? Do you know the guy's name, or don't you?"

"I'm sorry, but this club is for hotel guests and members only."

"This guy in the gray suit—did he meet anybody here?"

"I'll have to ask you to leave the health club if you're not hotel guests," I said firmly.

"Are you going to answer our question?" Greasy asked.

"I've got a good idea," I said. "I'll call our chief of security. You can ask him."

"She doesn't know anything," one man muttered to the other.

They gave one last look around the room and left.

I decided I'd better talk to someone in security, and Tina was closest. She was perched on the edge of a lounge chair animatedly chatting with the man with the brown hair. I opened the glass door and beckoned to her. She nodded and stood up.

As I walked back to the office I noticed that Mr. Kamara was accepting a tray from Floyd. Their heads were together, and Mr. Kamara was complaining about something. Floyd looked unhappy. I supposed, from what I'd heard, that Mr. Kamara was awfully difficult to please.

He was such a predictable person, always doing the same thing over and over. Some people really fall into ruts in their lives. Since coming to work at the health club I'd noticed that each afternoon, around three o'clock, Mr. Jones came to the health club, chatted with Mr. Kamara, and left. Then about a half hour later Mr. Kamara called room service for something to eat, and

Floyd brought it. In a little while Mr. Kamara would go for another swim, then leave the club. During the late evening hours he'd be back for another swim. According to Deeley, Mr. Kamara had a morning swim and Mr. Jones usually joined him for coffee by the pool. Same dull pattern every day. Didn't he ever want to do something more interesting?

Tina joined me in the office. "His name is Kurt Quentin Fraiser. He's from New Jersey, and he's here on computer business, but all he can talk about is how much he hates Houston and how dangerous the city is, which shows a decided lack of social perception and ability to relate to the inner needs of others."

"Why does he feel so horrible about Houston?"

"His wallet got lifted while he was out with some business associates last night."

"You told me that happened to a lot of the guests here."

"I know, but they can't blame the Ridley, because it doesn't happen at the hotel, and they shouldn't blame Houston, because pickpockets are at work in every city of the world."

"Did he call the police?"

"Of course, and had to go through all the work of informing credit-card companies, which is a big nuisance. Which reminds me—speaking of cards, if he's going to be here all week, then what about his card? It should be—"

"Tina," I interrupted, "listen for a minute. There were two men here asking questions about Mr. Jones and who he was and if he met anyone here. They didn't belong here. I think you should find out what they're up to."

Immediately Tina was all business. "What did they look like? Give me a good description."

I thought hard, trying to remember their faces. "They were about so-so tall. One was kind of yucky, the other was a greaseball."

Tina rolled her eyes. "Color eyes? Color hair? What were they wearing?"

"Oh," I said, and told her what little I could remember. She immediately trotted toward the hotel.

A woman poked her head in the doorway. "My little girl dropped her doll in the pool," she said. "If I dive for it I'll ruin my hair. Can you fish it out?"

"Certainly," I told her. I took the long pole with the round, taut net and followed her to the shallow end of the pool. It took just a few minutes to fish out the doll. The little girl grabbed her baby and hugged it.

"Say thank-you," her mother said.

But the child turned and ran away. Her mother strolled after her.

"Some children have no manners," Mrs. Bandini clucked.

I saw some leaves floating at the side of the pool, so I used the net to fish them out.

"When it's windy the leaves from outside fall into the pool," Mrs. Larabee said. "Wait till it's windy. You'll get a lot of work fishing out leaves."

I looked up at the ficus tree nearby. "The trees in here don't seem to drop many of their leaves."

Mrs. Bandini and Mrs. Larabee chuckled as though they shared a great joke. "That's because the ficus trees aren't real," Mrs. Bandini said.

I reached out and touched the tree's trunk. "It feels real."

"Oh, the trunk and branches are from a real tree. That's what makes them look like they're live ficus trees. But if you look closely you can see that the leaves are silk and glued on." Mrs. Larabee looked smug. "Most people would think what you thought, but we know better."

I glanced around at the other plants. "Are the others fake too?"

"Don't say 'fake.' " Mrs. Bandini leaned forward, her voice barely above a whisper. " 'Fake' is for cheap plants. Say 'artificial.' It has more quality, and believe me, you couldn't touch these ficus trees for under $298 apiece."

"The other plants are real," Mrs. Larabee said. "But ficus are hard to grow inside and they make a terrible mess with leaves all over the place, so that's why these are artificial."

I had my mouth open to ask another question, but Tina suddenly burst through the hotel door and loped to where I was standing. "Liz!" she said. "The manager is furious, and Lamar is furious, and you're a witness."

"A witness? To what?"

"To the thieves," she said. "A couple of hours ago someone stole two of the hotel's valuable antique sofas!"

5

I have never been ordered to march myself to the principal's office, but I could always imagine how horrifying the experience must be. Being sent to the Ridley Hotel manager's office was just as terrifying. I mentally practiced what I would do and say. I would smile graciously, charmingly, and introduce myself with dignity. After all, what was I so scared of? I hadn't done anything.

As I entered the office three men slowly rose and stared at me.

The office was large enough to have a sofa-and-chairs-conversation grouping at one end and a desk at the other. The walls and upholstery were in blues and corals and grays, all brightened by the glass window-wall at one side. A huge bouquet of real flowers was at one end of the desk, and another bouquet on the coffee table in front of the sofa. The flower tones mirrored the soft room colors.

So did one of the men. He wore a light wool gray suit with a coral-and-gray-striped tie. I assumed he was the manager, so I said, "I'm Mary Elizabeth Rafferty, sir." I held out a hand and took a large step forward, banging my shin into the coffee table and toppling the small vase of flowers. Deftly I caught them, righted them, and held out my hand again.

He didn't shake my hand. He just made an impatient motion, as though I were a fly he'd like to shoo away, and sat down. The other two men immediately sat down. Nobody asked me, but I sat down too.

"You know Mr. Boudry," the manager said, "and this is Detective Jarvis from the Houston Police Department."

I nodded to Lamar, whose solemn facial expression didn't change, and to the detective, who didn't seem to fit either in the chair or in the dark-blue suit he was wearing. His shoulders were as broad as a football player's, and what was left of his hair was sun-bleached.

"I'm sorry, but no one has ever told me *your* name," I said to the manager.

"I am Mr. Lewis Parmegan," he said.

"How do you do, Mr. Parmegan. I'm Mary Eli—"

"So I have been informed," he said. "I have also been informed that you arrived at the Ridley at the same time as the men who came to pick up the sofas."

His eyes darted like little spears in Lamar's direction. A muscle in Lamar's chin twitched. He must have been terribly upset.

"They claimed they had an order to clean the sofas," I said. "I don't understand what happened. Did someone steal the sofas from them?"

Detective Jarvis leaned toward me. "It was a bogus operation," he said. "The men who took the sofas simply posed as cleaners. They had no order to clean the sofas. They used the trick to steal them."

"That's awful!" I said.

"Can you give us descriptions of the men?" he asked.

I leaned back in my chair and thought a moment. "Yes," I said. "I didn't pay much attention to the driver of the truck, so I can't tell you anything about him. There were four men who came inside the hotel with me. Two were just ho-hum, one was kind of a yuck, and the other was about an eight."

Detective Jarvis looked up from the pad he had balanced on his knee and licked the end of his pencil. "What does that mean?"

"Be specific," Lamar snapped.

"Like color of hair and that kind of stuff?"

"Exactly."

I wish Fran had been with me. He probably would have remembered. I had to think hard. "Okay. Two of the men were the kind who show up in a group picture at a company picnic and somebody says, 'Who are those guys?' only nobody remembers that they were even there at all. That's what they looked like."

Mr. Parmegan gave a sigh. "Height? Weight?"

"The same."

They all stared at me, and I added, "I mean, who'd notice? Kind of average."

The detective shifted, and his chair creaked. "How about the other two? Anything you could identify about them?"

"Let's see—the man with the clipboard. He was kind of a dandruffy type with a moustache that should have been sent to the cleaners. Jowls too."

"What color moustache?" Detective Jarvis asked.

"Dirty." He just looked at me, so I tried to elaborate. "Maybe brown-dirty. I can't remember."

"Anything else?"

"He was the yuck," I said.

"How about the fourth man? He's the eight?"

"Right."

Mr. Parmegan shook his head. "Wait a minute. We established there were only four inside the building, not eight."

"Eight, meaning on a scale of one to ten," I told him. I was getting warmed up now. "He was about six one, with sandy hair that curled up just a smidgen where it was long on his neck, and a dimple in the middle of his chin, and blue eyes, and broad shoulders, and his ears were just a little bit pointy, which was kind of cute."

"Weight?" Detective Jarvis was writing as fast as he could.

"Perfect."

Lamar scowled at me. "We are asking for specifics."

"Specifically, I couldn't tell you. I didn't weigh him. I just fell under him."

Detective Jarvis looked as puzzled as Mr. Parmegan, so I hurried to explain what had happened.

"Just what did you hear the men say?" the detective asked, so I told him what I remembered.

"Did you see Mr. Boudry sign the order form?"

The manager was glaring at Lamar as though the whole thing were Lamar's fault. I felt sorry for him. I said, "No, I didn't."

"Thank you, Miss Rafferty. You may go now," the manager said.

But I wasn't ready to go. "Don't blame Mr. Boudry," I said. "The men couldn't have stolen the sofas if Mr. Parmegan didn't leave for lunch at the exact same time every day."

"What?" Mr. Parmegan's mouth popped open and stayed open.

"Sure," I said. "Their plan wouldn't work if Mr. Parmegan had been available. They had to know he wouldn't be on hand. I'd guess that somebody in the hotel, who knew Mr. Parmegan's schedule, worked it all out."

Detective Jarvis licked his pencil point again and smiled at me. "Good thinking," he said.

But Mr. Parmegan scowled at Mr. Boudry so hard that his forehead almost met the end of his nose, and his words peppered the room like BB shot. "Mr. Boudry is one of those who know my daily schedule."

"So does nearly everyone who works at the Ridley," Lamar answered.

"Especially Mr. Parmegan," I added.

"Thanks for your help, Mary Elizabeth," Detective Jarvis said. "We may want you to look at some mug shots later, but for now you can get back to work."

Again I thought about that gap in the walls outside the pool area. There didn't seem much point in telling Detective Jarvis, since the gap had nothing to do with the theft of the sofas, so I kept my mouth shut.

Lamar and Mr. Parmegan didn't notice when I left the office. They were too busy studying each other with deep suspicion.

I hurried back to the health club. Since we didn't have a lifeguard, it wasn't mandatory that someone be on duty every single minute, but the guests liked it better if one of us was there to smile at them and hand them a towel as they checked in, and Lamar liked it better if we checked names and faces with the photo-ID cards and made sure that no one sneaked in.

But I hadn't needed to worry. Art Mart was slouched down in the desk chair, admiring his long, muscular legs, which were stretched out in front of him. He barely glanced up as I came into the office.

"Look, I'm sorry I had to be gone, but it wasn't my fault," I began.

Art just slammed his chair upright and snapped, "I know where you were."

"Do you know what happened?"

"Of course I know. Everybody in the hotel knows by this time."

"Oh," I said.

Art gave a wicked chuckle. "And they even got the security chief to sign for it! That's terrific!"

"I don't think it's so funny," I said. "Lamar is very embarrassed about it."

For the first time Art's eyes met mine. "He should be embarrassed. For all any of us know, he was in on it."

"No! I don't believe that!"

He slowly stood up and stretched, rippling all the way down. I wasn't impressed. Mrs. Zellendorf's cat can do the same thing. "Now that you're here, you can take over," he said. "I'm off and won't be back until tomorrow A.M."

"Okay."

"Don't forget to clean the tiles and pick up the towels," he said.

I had to clamp my teeth together until they hurt to keep from reminding him that I hadn't forgot yet, and he knew it.

He sauntered from the indoor pool area toward the hotel, stopping to smile and ripple at two good-looking women who were lounging near the Jacuzzi.

Mr. Kamara passed him on his way to the pool. They said something to each other, and I could practically see sparks. What was the matter with Art? He was always preaching to me about keeping the hotel guests happy. Mr. Kamara growled something and belly-flopped into the water, swimming back and forth, back and forth, without stopping or paying any more attention to Art, who wheeled and stomped out of the club as though he were trying to make dents in the floor.

For the moment the club was fairly quiet. Pauly was stuffing his face at a table near the pool, but his grandmother and Mrs. Larabee were nowhere in sight. I checked and tidied the women's dressing area and opened the door of the sauna.

There sat Mrs. Bandini and Mrs. Larabee, the steam swirling around them. Mrs. Larabee was wearing her black racer bathing suit, but Mrs. Bandini was wrapped in a towel with soggy blue tennis shoes on her feet.

She smiled at me from under a bouffant, plastic shower cap. "Come in, come in, and shut the door," she said as though she were in her own kitchen. "Tell us what happened."

I shut the door, but the steam made my eyes water. "Some thieves claiming to be from a cleaning company took the two big sofas in the lobby. Only they weren't from a cleaning company. They stole them."

"My stars!" Mrs. Bandini turned to Mrs. Larabee. "Those beautiful silver-and-cream sofas! Imagine that!"

"They're not silver and cream. They're goldish and pinkish," Mrs. Larabee said.

"Silver and cream, but does it matter what color? We're talking about the fact that they're stolen!"

"If they're stolen, they have to identify them. And how can they identify them if they don't know what color they are?"

I mumbled something and hurried out of the sauna. Strands of my hair were already beginning to damply plaster themselves on my ears and cheeks.

I strolled back to the desk. With no immediate jobs to

take care of, I could go through the photo-ID cards again.

The cards were alphabetized when they were put into the file box. I made a little song in my head about the last names as I mentally recorded them with the photos I was looking at. Durstan, Effendale, Ender, Fallon, Fox, Fraiser, Garnett—

Fraiser? I went back to his card. Kurt Quentin Fraiser. A good-looking guy with brown hair. I thought Tina had said his card wasn't in here.

I picked up the phone and rang the security office.

"Yo," Lamar answered.

"This is Liz. Is Tina there?"

"What's wrong?"

"Nothing. I just need to ask Tina about one of the photo-ID cards."

"Something wrong with the card?"

"No."

"You want to tell Tina about some good-looking dude. Well, do it when you're both off duty."

"But I also want to ask her about two guys who—"

Lamar had cut the connection, so I sighed and hung up, too, once again marveling at how much he knew. He was really a good chief of security, and it wasn't fair that Mr. Parmegan was blaming him for the sofas being stolen.

I leaned my chin on my hands, and my elbows on the desk, gazing out the window between my desk and the pool and trying to think. Something was peculiar about those photo-ID cards, but what was it? I couldn't zero in on the problem, because of Pauly Canelli.

The precrowd club seemed peaceful. Even the fake— uh, artificial—trees looked drowsy. Two women were snoozing next to the pool, their towels pulled over them like blankets, and Mr. Kamara was chugging awake back and forth across the pool, as regular as a windup boat.

But Pauly wasn't peaceful. He had finished his gigantic snack and was obviously bored and looking for something interesting to do. I watched his eyes widen and his lips stretch into a wicked grin as he spotted the pair of sleeping women, and it wasn't hard to tell what he had in mind. He slowly got up from his chair, peeled off the T-shirt he'd been wearing, and began an exaggerated tiptoe toward the women.

I slid out of my chair and zipped to the office doorway. By the time I reached it he was already crouching into the cannonball position.

"Pauly Canelli!" I yelled. "Don't you dare!"

My shout startled Pauly. Instead of stepping back and behaving himself, without looking or caring, he flung his round, tight little cannonball body smack into the pool.

And smack on top of Mr. Kamara, who sank straight to the bottom.

I felt as though I were in a slow-motion movie. I ran to the edge of the pool, tugging off my shoes and flinging them aside, then dived. It seemed to take forever, because while I was doing this my eyes were on Mr. Kamara. He didn't move. Obviously Pauly had knocked him out.

My momentum carried me across the pool in a matter of seconds. I grabbed Mr. Kamara's chin with both hands and pushed hard against the bottom of the pool. We rose to the top and I flipped on my side. One of my arms was under his chin. I used the other in a side stroke to help propel us to shallow water.

Both of the women who had been Pauly's targets were already in the water. They helped me pull Mr. Kamara from the pool. Mr. Kamara helped too. By this time he was choking and sputtering and conscious again.

He sat on the edge of the pool and rubbed his head.

"I'll call a doctor," I said.

"No. A doctor not necessary," he said.

"I didn't mean to jump on you," Pauly said, his voice quivering. He reminded me of the huge-eyed lemurs in the night-animal section of the zoo.

"That is what happened?" Mr. Kamara asked. He stared at Pauly and mumbled something in his native tongue. I didn't ask for a translation. His tone of voice told me all I needed to know.

Pauly's lower lip curled out. "It's her fault," he said, pointing at me. "She yelled at me and scared me. That's why I didn't see you."

One of the women said, "What a rude little boy. I heard her tell you earlier not to splash water on people. That's what you were planning to do to us, wasn't it?"

The other woman pointed at me and said to Mr. Kamara, "She dived right in and pulled you out."

"Thank you," he said to me.

"Thank them too," I answered, smiling at the women. "They helped me."

Mr. Kamara struggled to his feet and staggered over to the chair on which his robe was neatly folded and hung. He pulled on his robe and stepped into his thongs.

"Are you sure you're all right?" I asked him.

"Yes. All right."

I turned to Pauly, brushing back the dripping hair from my eyes. "As for you—I am not going to allow you back in the pool for the rest of the day."

"Not all his fault," Mr. Kamara said. He put a hand on Pauly's shoulder. "Too much to think about. I not pay attention."

"Is something wrong, Mr. Kamara? Can I do anything to help?"

For a long moment he looked at me, and I saw something flicker in his eyes. I wouldn't have been surprised if a light bulb had appeared over his head, like in the old cartoon shows. He gave a little bow and grinned, but oddly the grin seemed to be more for himself than for me. "Ah, yes. You can help."

He tugged his robe more tightly around himself, turned sharply, and wobbled from the pool area to the door to the hotel.

I wished I could take back my words. I wished that I could call out, "Wait, Mr. Kamara! I didn't mean it!" For just an instant, before he turned away, I had glimpsed an almost evil expression of triumph on his face. I didn't know what plan Mr. Kamara had in mind, but I was sure I was going to regret being any part of it.

6

Mrs. Bandini apologized over and over again for Pauly's actions. When he complained that I had ordered him out of the pool for the rest of the day, she said I was perfectly right, and by pure coincidence it was time they were getting home anyway. Pauly made a face at me as they left.

I changed to an extra pair of pink shorts and a club T-shirt, which fortunately I kept in my locker, wrote out a detailed report in the day's log, and called Lamar to tell him what had happened.

"I'm a little worried about Mr. Kamara," I said.

"I'll check on him," he told me. "You were right to inform me."

Lamar seemed to be calm and controlled again. I was glad he wasn't still so upset. For a "fun health club" in a "relaxing, restful hotel," we were pretty far off base.

I had no sooner put down the desk telephone than Detective Jarvis called. "Mr. Parmegan told me your working hours," he said. "Could you make it downtown to the police station tomorrow morning to look at mug shots?"

"Sure," I said. "What time?"

"How about nine o'clock?"

"Just tell me how to get there."

"Do you have a car?"

Old Junk Bucket. "I guess you could call it a car."

He gave me directions to the HPD main station on Riesner, and I carefully wrote them down.

I wished I could talk to Tina. I wished I could talk to Fran. I wished I could switch the hotel's piped-in music to station KLEF. I'd feel a lot better if I could conduct an orchestra through an entire symphony. A symphony is so beautifully orderly. No klutzy people or stupid mistakes or deep black swimming pools. The pools in a symphony are bright spots of sound that trill or call or beat or blast or soar, each of them different, each of them woven together by a conductor with a baton.

None of my wishes came true. Instead, more people than I'd ever seen in the health club began to straggle in. It was all I could do to unobtrusively check ID cards and hand out towels and smiles. They must have been with the big convention Art Mart had told me about. Meetings were over, and they were ready to relax.

Finally, for a few moments, the office was empty. I glanced through the window and surveyed the indoor section of the health club. The Jacuzzi was loaded. A ring of heads and shoulders encircled the bubbles, reminding me of one of those battery games in which a ring of fish keep opening and closing their mouths, and you have to try to catch them.

Just beyond the Jacuzzi Fran was delivering a tray of drinks to four hairy-chested, potbellied men. Fran! I had to catch him.

I tugged down the back of my pink shorts and sauntered from the office, smiling and surveying and trying to look both official and efficient. As I passed Fran I murmured, "We need to get together."

He straightened and beamed at me. "I knew you'd eventually be attracted to me."

I felt myself blushing, knowing he'd been overheard.

One of the men, who'd been lazily scratching his chest, stopped and studied me.

"Be quiet, Fran," I said. "That's not what I meant. I just have to talk to you about—about—well, you know what."

"But of course," Fran answered, trying to look mysterious. "The usual time. The usual place." He swung his empty tray to his shoulder, picked up the signed check, and walked briskly toward the door to the hotel.

"Excuse me," I said to the row of assorted eyes at the table. Nervously, I stepped back and skidded in a puddle of water. I reached out, grabbing at anything to keep from falling, and found myself gripping the slender trunk of a fake ficus tree. The ficus and I spun clockwise, but I managed to stay on my feet.

I caught my balance, brushed myself off nonchalantly, as though I performed this trick every day, and stared hard at the tree. It had turned with me. I know it had. Yet the base of the tree, with its level layer of wooden chips, looked undisturbed. I tried to pick up one of the chips, but it was glued in place. Well, of course it would be. The whole thing was fake, wasn't it?

Embarrassed by my clumsiness, and as red as those misguided lobsters sunning overlong around the outside section of the pool, I dutifully walked my beat around the pool, outside and in, then dashed into the office to catch the telephone.

"You've got a crowd this afternoon," Tina said.

"Oh, Tina, I'm glad you called. What did you find out about those men who had been in the club?"

"Nothing," she said. "I couldn't find them."

"They left in an awful hurry," I said. "That should prove they didn't belong here. That and the fact that their faces weren't on any of the cards."

"Don't try to make a mystery out of them." Tina gave a loud yawn. "A lot of strange people wander in and out of a hotel."

"But they asked nosy questions about Mr. Jones. Shouldn't we do something about it?"

"There's nothing to do. Except, I guess, if you see them again, let me know right away."

"Did Lamar tell you that I tried to reach you earlier?"

"No. Anything important?"

"Yes," I said. "That guy's card. That Kurt Quentin Fraiser. It's back in the file."

"Forget him," Tina said. "I have."

"But, Tina—"

"I've been thinking about it," Tina said. "There's no point in wasting time flirting with men from out of town. It's an exercise in frustration and could eventually lead to a lower self-image if I'm not careful. I need a really positive self-image."

"Tina—"

"I'm tired of being a poor nobody," Tina said. "And it's hard waiting to be rich and famous. Did I tell you that I'm going to be famous too?"

"Probably," I said.

"Of course, if anyone really super comes in, I might make an exception."

"Tina, about the cards—"

"Lamar's coming back. I've got to tour the lobby. Talk to you later," Tina said, and hung up.

I stared at the telephone for a couple of minutes. If Tina weren't concerned about a card that was missing, then wasn't, maybe I shouldn't be either. I couldn't help it. The whole thing made me feel uncomfortable.

A second wave of guests came into the hotel as the first wave dressed and went out for late dinners. Very few people wanted to swim outside at this hour, so the inside section of the pool was crowded with laughing, splashing bodies. Just tidying up after all those people was a full-time job, and most of them couldn't read. I mean, people kept taking glasses into the Jacuzzi, even though right over their heads was a decorative sign asking them not to; and one out-of-shape businessman after another belly-slapped the water right under the sign that said NO DIVING IN THE POOL, PLEASE. Maybe whoever had painted the signs shouldn't have included the word *please.* No one seemed to take the rules seriously.

By eleven o'clock, when the last guests had been politely edged out of the club, I had picked up at least two dozen towels from the floor and bench in front of the towel hamper, and made a collection of items that had been left behind and could be claimed in the office: two pairs of sunglasses, a paperback romance novel, four combs, one funky earring, and a very skimpy top of a bathing suit. It was certainly small enough. I could see how the owner could misplace it—even when it was being worn.

Fran came in one door of the office as I stepped through the other. His hair was neatly combed, and his smile was as bright as the bowl of daisies he thrust toward me.

"Thank you!" I said. "They're beautiful!"

"And practically fresh too," Fran said. "The people in 912 only had them two days before they checked out."

"Secondhand daisies?"

"Bet you never heard of that before, huh?" His smile didn't waver. I put the bowl on the desk as he added, "Where to?"

"Sit down," I said.

"I thought we were going somewhere to talk."

"We can talk right here."

As he sat in the extra office chair his shoulders slumped just a little, his coat wrinkled, and his cowlick sprang into action. It was the most vivid case of disappointment I'd ever seen.

I sat across the desk from him and leaned forward, keeping my voice low. "Listen, Fran. This is business. Important business. I need to talk to you about the crimes going on at the hotel."

"You need to talk to Lamar, not to me."

I shook my head. "No. I don't have any real facts to give Lamar, just feelings."

"I can't do much about your feelings. I've tried."

"For one thing," I said, "some of the cards in the file are missing, then they turn up again."

He blinked a couple of times. "That's a crime?"

"I don't know what it is. It's strange, and it must mean something." He continued to look puzzled, so I said, "And then there's all the valuable stuff that's stolen from the hotel."

"Like the two sofas?"

"The sofas make the third thing. Those so-called cleaning men didn't take all the paintings and silver and stuff that Lamar told us has been disappearing."

"So we've got three crimes? I don't see—"

"Four. Don't forget the meat. Lamar said roasts and turkeys were disappearing from the kitchen."

For a few minutes Fran closed his eyes, nodded sagely,

and kept murmuring, "Um-hum, um-hum," while I waited eagerly for what he would say. Finally he opened his eyes, looked at me, and said, "You realize that none of this makes a bit of sense."

"But it has to!" I wailed.

"How? As far as we know, the men who said they were from a cleaning company had never been seen in the hotel before. There'd be no way they could take the smaller valuables. And if they walked into the kitchens and stole some of the roasts, they'd certainly be seen by some of the chefs. Do you know how many people work in the Ridley kitchens?"

He picked up a pencil and tore a sheet of paper off the pad next to the telephone. On it he drew three circles. "Here are your crimes," he said. "You can see that none of them is related to the others in any way."

I reached over and drew a fourth circle. The circles now formed a crescent shape. "Don't forget the photo-ID cards."

"What kind of a crazy criminal would steal cards from the photo-ID file and then bring them back?"

"Kurt Quentin Fraiser had his wallet stolen."

Fran stood up, leaned toward me so that our noses were almost touching, and said, "Who is Quirt Kenton Fraiser, and what has his wallet got to do with anything?"

I leaned back and sighed. "I wish I knew."

His voice became soothing. "You've been working very hard today, haven't you?"

"Don't patronize me, Fran."

"Of course not," he said. "Let's go somewhere and get ice cream and talk about Quirk Frentin Kaiser's wallet."

"I want to go home."

"Good idea. I'd like that," he said. "Do you have plenty of ice cream there?"

I picked up the telephone and dialed the security office. Tina answered.

"Tina," I said, "you told me that Quirk—uh—Kurt Quentin Fraiser had his wallet stolen."

"Who? Oh . . . yeah. I remember. Yes, he did."

"And his card was missing at the time."

"Was it?"

"It must have been."

"So?"

"So what about the others who've had their wallets stolen by pickpockets? What about their cards?"

"I don't know," she said. "I haven't checked on their cards."

"Then maybe we'd better."

"It's all past tense. I don't see how we can," Tina told me. "Anyhow, it's past time for my shift to end, and I'm leaving as soon as Lamar gets back to the office. Why don't we just sleep on the idea and see if anything else develops?"

"That's just an excuse to get out of doing anything tonight," I told her.

"You're wrong," she said. " 'Sleeping on it' is a valid way of allowing the subconscious mind to wrestle with a problem. It's been verified by countless researchers."

"Okay, Tina," I said. "See you tomorrow afternoon." I replaced the receiver and turned back to Fran. "Does it make sense now?"

"Yes," Fran said. "You'll be glad to know that I've stopped worrying about your mental condition."

I had to smile at him. He looked like an elf that hoped he wouldn't be stepped on. "Then why don't we get the ice cream?" I asked.

None of the ice-cream shops were open, so we ended up buying two pints of double chocolate chip and a bag of plastic spoons in an all-night Randall's supermarket. We sat in Fran's car in the store's parking lot—under an arc light that turned our lips purple—ate the ice cream, and talked.

We didn't talk about crime at the Ridley. We talked about ourselves. Fran had dreams too. He told me how intensely he had wanted to be an international ski champion and how hard he had worked until three years ago when his family had moved from Denver, Colorado, to Houston, where the only deep snow comes on Christmas cards.

"You don't have to be tall to be a skiing champion," Fran said. He looked off into space for a few minutes, and a glob of ice cream fell from his spoon back into the carton. I knew he was seeing himself soaring out over a ski jump, in perfect harmony with the earth and the sky.

I told Fran about my dream of conducting an orchestra. He listened seriously and said that he could understand. He wiggled over so that our shoulders touched. He wiped a smudge of ice cream off my chin, and with his spoon he scooped up a blob that had landed on my T-shirt.

"Sorry," I said. "I tend to be clumsy. I'm always embarrassing myself."

"Don't be embarrassed," he said. "You're beautiful enough to get away with a little clumsiness."

"Me? Beautiful?"

"Of course," Fran said. He took my empty ice cream carton, tossed them both in the backseat, put his arms around my shoulders, and kissed me.

I liked his kiss. I wanted to snuggle right into it. Obviously, skiing was not the only thing that Fran was good at. But a message of reason kept poking me. This wouldn't work. I couldn't date a guy who was four inches shorter than me! And what about my plan to hold out for what I wanted—for the best? If I let this go on, Fran would be hurt.

I squirmed all the way to the car door and reached behind my back for the handle. "It's late," I said. "Mom might decide to call me again. I'd better get home."

Fran didn't say anything. He just kept looking at me.

"Listen," I said. "We're friends. Okay? I don't think we should let romance get mixed up in our friendship."

"If I were a few inches taller, would you feel the same way?"

What could I say? That I have another dream? That I know somewhere out there is a handsome guy who is so tall that I'll have to look up to him?

"Please, Fran," I murmured, and wished with all my heart that Fran could have been that guy.

He sat up a little straighter, gave a shrug, and said, "I'll follow you home to make sure you get there all right."

"Thanks," I said. "I don't live far from here."

"I know." He smiled. "We can do this again—the ice-cream part, that is."

"Sure," I said, and climbed out of his car. Why did life have to be so darned mixed up?

The next morning I was too busy to think about anything except getting to the police station on time. I left Old Junk Bucket in the parking lot, hoping no one would think he was evidence in an accident case and tow him away. I had dressed in a light-blue tailored shirt and denim skirt, hoping to look so dignified that no one would mistake me for a criminal.

I had never been to a police station, and I suppose that I expected a scene out of one of the television cop shows. But inside the building everything was orderly. Some well-dressed people, carrying briefcases, strode briskly through the small lobby and down corridors as though they knew exactly where they were going and had a great deal of work to get done. A few people, not so well dressed, who didn't seem to know their destinations, were directed by a guard at an information booth. I quickly looked around, but no one was dragging in a screaming junkie, and nobody was yelling threats at anyone else. I'd have to remember to tell Fran that this was nothing like the shows on TV.

Someone came up beside me, and I heard the deep voice of Detective Jarvis. "You're right on time, Mary Elizabeth," he said. "Come upstairs with me."

We stepped into an elevator with two men dressed in paint-splattered overalls and caps and a woman who looked like an ad in *Business Journal.* She gave me a sharp, speculative glance over the top rim of her glasses. It made me feel peculiar, so I leaned toward her.

"I'm not being arrested," I whispered.

The men grinned at me. *"¡Bueno!"* one of them said, but the woman narrowed her eyes and pulled back behind her glasses the way a turtle pulls back inside his shell. I died until the elevator door opened.

"Watch your step," Detective Jarvis said, leading the way from the elevator. I stumbled into the hallway after him.

He took me into a room in which a number of large scrapbooks were piled on a long wooden table. He pulled back a plastic-and-chrome chair, its legs squeaking against the linoleum-covered floor.

"Sit here," he said, "and carefully go through these books. See if you recognize any of the faces. I've got a couple of things to do, and I'll be back in a few minutes." He walked out into the hall, leaving the door wide open.

The books, with their worn, heavy covers, smelled of stale cigarettes. I squirmed into a more comfortable position on the chair, opened the first book, and plunged into a whirlpool of faces. Page after page of faces. Each of them was different, yet pretty soon they all began to look alike. How in the world would I ever be able to find or recognize the two faces I remembered from the sofa theft?

Detective Jarvis swung around the door frame, leaning into the room. "Anything yet?"

"No," I answered.

"Stick with it," he said.

"Did Lamar Boudry do this?" I asked.

"Yesterday."

"Did he find any of the guys?"

"We'll talk about it later. I don't want to influence you."

So I went back to slowly turning pages, one book after another. I tried so hard, but again, all the faces began to blend together.

Until I suddenly saw someone I knew. I was so surprised that I let out a yelp.

Immediately Detective Jarvis was back in the room. He walked behind me and stared down at the book. "Got one?" he asked. He sounded surprised.

I shook my head. "Not one of the sofa thieves," I told him, jabbing a finger at one of the pictures. "But this man—I know him! He comes to the health club every day. His name is C. L. Jones."

Detective Jarvis pulled up another small chrome chair and sat in it, spilling over on both sides. He looked at the picture and at me with a strange expression on his face.

"C. L. Jones, you say."

He paused, and I asked, "Is something the matter?"

"It is to Mr. Jones," he said. "Early this morning someone walking through a field off Highway 280 found the
remains of a car that had been on fire. Inside the car was
what was left of a body. One license plate on the car was
intact, so from that we traced the car's owner." He
paused, ran his tongue over his teeth, and shifted his
weight so that the chair cracked and creaked, before he
added, "We think that the body in the car is the man you
call Mr. C. L. Jones."

7

"Judging from the automobile tracks leading from the highway into the field," Detective Jarvis said, "it looked to the officer who wrote up the report that the driver had been speeding, hit a tree, and the car exploded. However, because of Mr. Jones's past record we're investigating other possibilities."

"What other possibilities could there be?" I thought a moment and shivered. "Except for murder."

"Stay put," Detective Jarvis told me. "I'll be right back." It didn't take long. He soon returned carrying a folder. He sat down again and opened the folder on the desk, reading through it quickly.

"Suppose you tell me what you know about Mr. Jones," Detective Jarvis said.

"Is Jones his real name?"

"Just one of the many names he used."

"You said he had a record. What kind of a record?"

"Theft, burglary, pickpocketing. No armed robbery, though. Couple of probated sentences. Three short prison terms. Early parole each time."

While Jarvis took notes, I told him everything I knew

about Mr. Jones, which wasn't much, just how he came to
the health club a couple of times a day and met with Mr.
Kamara. And how those two men had come asking about
Mr. Jones, but I wouldn't tell them anything.

"Can you describe the men?" Detective Jarvis asked.

"Not very well. One was a real nothing. The other was
a 'before' picture in a shampoo commercial."

He sighed patiently and shook his head.

"No good, huh?" I asked. "Okay. I'll try to remember
the description I gave to Tina. Both of them were about
my height and kind of stocky. Jowly too. One had black
hair. He's the one I called a greaseball. Both of them real
minus types."

"Let's get away from your scale of masculine charm.
Have you got any idea how old the men were?" he asked.

"Old," I said.

He looked surprised. "Sixty? Sixty-five?"

"I didn't say 'ancient.' I meant maybe about forty."

"You said they were wearing business suits. What
color?"

"Dark. Maybe brown or blue or charcoal or whatever."

"Any identifying marks?"

"You mean like designer labels?"

"I mean on the men themselves! Tattoos? Moles?
Birthmarks?"

I thought hard, then shook my head. "I would think
that being greasy and incredibly ugly would be identifying marks."

Detective Jarvis closed his eyes for a moment. Then he
said, "Would you have recognized their photos if you'd
seen them in the books you've been looking through?"

"Yes," I said. "I think so."

"Then how about checking out the rest of the books.
How many more there? Two?"

"Okay," I said, "as long as I can get to work in time."

He stood, shoving back his chair, which seemed to be permanently dented. "I'm going to have to leave the building. I have an appointment concerning another case. If you see any pictures you recognize, just tell the sergeant at the desk in the next room—the plump guy with the gray hair." He smiled at me. "You're probably getting hungry, aren't you? I'll send in a hamburger and milk shake for you. Chocolate okay?"

"Great!" I said, and then I got this scary thought. "Is it jail food?"

"No," he said. "It's from the hamburger stand around the corner. It's cop food."

Cop food. That was almost as interesting. It made the time go faster, but it didn't help with the pictures. Finally I closed the last book, looked at my watch, and went to tell the sergeant. His desk was a mess of papers and forms and even some photographs.

He nodded. "Thanks for helping."

"I wasn't much help. I couldn't find any of the faces I was looking for."

"Never mind. You gave us something to go on with the Jones case."

I had to ask. "Was Lamar Boudry able to identify any of the photos when he was in here yesterday?"

The sergeant shook his head. "No. He drew a blank too."

He picked up a stack of photographs and thumped their edges on the desk, trying to get them aligned. Then he shoved them to the far right corner, just next to me. I automatically glanced down at the photo on top.

"But you've found one of the men in the business suits."

"No." He looked puzzled.

I pointed to the man in the photograph. He was wearing a hat, but I would have recognized him anyway. "This man," I said. "He's one of the two who came into the health club to ask about Mr. Jones."

"Is that so?" He became very interested. "You're sure of that?"

"Yes, I'm sure."

"Very interesting. Very interesting indeed." He reached for the phone and dialed.

"Why is it so interesting?"

"We suspect this perpetrator may have a tie-in with a branch of the syndicate in Miami."

He began talking to someone on the phone. I looked at my watch. I had to leave right this very minute and hope that traffic on the Katy Freeway was light so I could get to the Ridley on time. I hurried out of the room, down the hall, and managed to catch an open elevator.

Fortunately, I got to the hotel in time to change into my shorts and health-club T-shirt before three o'clock. I even had two minutes to spare, so I quickly tidied up the women's dressing room.

When I returned to the office, Art Mart had appeared. He was sitting behind the desk, his chin on his hands, staring glumly into space.

"Guess what?" I asked.

"It's about time you got here," he snapped, and stood up.

"I'm two minutes early."

"I'll give you a medal." He pulled his car keys out of the desk and squeezed around me.

"But guess what?"

"Don't say, 'guess what.' I hate it when people say 'guess what.'"

"Sorry," I said.

"So what is it?"

"I thought you didn't want me to—"

He clamped his teeth together and almost growled. "I just said I didn't want to hear—Oh, forget it. Have you got something I'm supposed to know, or haven't you?"

"I have," I said. "I just came from the police station."

He looked startled. "Were you able to ID the thieves?"

"No," I said, "but I saw—ID'd—somebody else. Mr. Jones. You know, the Mr. Jones who comes every day to the club?"

Art leaned on the desk and stared at me. "What about Mr. Jones?"

At last I had an interested audience. "I showed Mr. Jones's picture to Detective Jarvis, and Detective Jarvis told me they had found a burned-up car this morning, and the car belonged to Mr. Jones. In fact, there was a body in the car, so they think that was probably Mr. Jones."

Art straightened up and whistled. He looked kind of sick for a minute. "That's awful," he said.

I nodded. "Somebody ought to tell Mr. Kamara about it. I think that he and Mr. Jones were friends."

"Where'd you get that idea?" Art asked.

"Well, they were always talking together. Mr. Kamara isn't very friendly with anyone else."

"Mr. Kamara hasn't any friends," Art said.

I looked through the large glass window toward the inner pool. As usual, Mrs. Bandini and Mrs. Larabee were seated together. Pauly, thank goodness, was nowhere in sight. Just a few people were in the club at this time, but I could see Mr. Kamara in his favorite spot at the table behind the large potted palm tree.

"There's Mr. Kamara. I'd better go and tell him," I said.

"You'd better get to work," Art said. "The ladies' dressing room needs straightening, and naturally I can't go in there while guests are in the club."

"Deeley's still out sick?"

"That's right. So get to work. I'll tell Mr. Kamara."

"I guess that's more proper. After all, you're the one in charge."

"Glad you noticed," Art said, and left the office.

I would have known that Deeley wasn't back without Art Mart's mentioning it. The desk hadn't been straightened. It looked just the way I had left it. Even the note paper with the four circles on it lay next to the pad. As I looked at those circles again, an idea wiggled so deeply in my mind that I couldn't catch it. There was something about those four circles in that crescent shape. But what? No matter how hard I tried, the idea wouldn't come.

I couldn't just stand there, trying to catch an idea. I had work to do, so I went straight to the dressing room, then realized that I had tidied it when I changed clothes here a few minutes ago. I strolled back through the office and stood in the doorway, surveying the pool area. Art had gone. Mr. Kamara was nowhere in sight.

Mrs. Bandini called to me and gestured wildly with both arms, so I walked over to join her and Mrs. Larabee.

"What is going on?" she asked in a stage whisper loud enough to be heard in the hotel.

"We are not ones to eavesdrop," Mrs. Larabee said, "but there was a commotion we couldn't miss going on behind the potted palm."

I glanced in the direction of the palm. It was where Mr. Kamara had been sitting. "What kind of commotion?" I asked.

Mrs. Bandini lit up. "Mr. Martin came and said something to Mr. Kamara—that part we missed—then Mr.

Kamara dropped his coffee cup with a crash and shouted
something in his own language—which we are not familiar with—and Mr. Martin told him to calm down, but it
took him a while."

She stopped for breath, and Mrs. Larabee took up the
story. "Naturally, we wanted to see if we could help, so
we got up and looked around the palm, and Mr.
Kamara's face was kind of green. I spoke right up and
asked if I could get him a glass of water or something,
and he shouted at me."

"We don't know what he shouted," Mrs. Bandini said,
"but his tone of voice left nothing to our imaginations."

"We have rarely been so insulted," Mrs. Larabee said.
She folded her hands primly in her lap and looked indig-
nant.

Mrs. Bandini didn't waste time with attitudes. She
leaned forward and said, "So he marched right out of
here, and Mr. Martin left, too, and we thought maybe
you could tell us what was going on."

I pulled up a chair and sat down. The only other guests
in the club at this time were outdoors catching some rays.
Nobody needed my assistance at this moment. "I knew
Mr. Kamara would be upset when he heard the news."

"What news?" they asked in unison.

"The news about Mr. C. L. Jones."

I thought I'd have to explain who Mr. Jones was, but
they both knew. Mrs. Larabee nodded, and Mrs. Bandini
said, "That weasely little man who chats with Mr. Kamara
every day."

"Yes," I said. "I told Art Mart—uh, Mr. Martin—that
Mr. Kamara would be upset. He didn't think so, but I was
right."

"Upset about what?" Mrs. Larabee asked.

"This morning the police found a car that had burned

during the night. It was off Highway 288. One license plate was intact, so they traced the owner of the car. It was Mr. Jones's car. They also found what was left of a body inside the car. They think it might be Mr. Jones."

For about ten seconds Mrs. Bandini closed her eyes and murmured a very short prayer. Mrs. Larabee tried to look pious. Then they began talking at once.

"How did you find out?"

"How can they tell if it's Mr. Jones?"

"Was it murder?"

"How come we didn't see it on TV news?"

"Poor Mr. Kamara. If they were friends, it must have been a terrible shock."

Finally Mrs. Bandini put a restraining hand on Mrs. Larabee's arm, scooted forward so that our faces were almost touching, and said, "Mary Elizabeth, tell us the whole story."

So I did, all about the police station and the mug shots and everything.

"If he wanted a complete description of the men in the business suits, your detective should have asked us," Mrs. Bandini said.

"You saw the men? You can remember them?"

"Of course," she said. "They came into the club right after I mentioned to you how very much you and my tall, handsome grandson, Eric Canelli, would like each other. And then you walked toward the door, so we watched you and saw the men. As a matter of fact the shorter one with the mole on the side of his face was wearing a pinstriped charcoal Louis Roth suit like the one my son-in-law, Jerry, bought at a sale at Sakowitz just last month. I commented upon it at the time, didn't I?"

"Distinctly," Mrs. Larabee said. "And I remember remarking that your son-in-law looks better in blue because of his complexion, which tends to look sallow in the winter."

"You saw Jerry when he was trying to get over the flu," Mrs. Bandini said. "He was sick, and Rose was sick, and it was a terrible week. Other than that week, he never looks sallow."

"Would you like to talk to Detective Jarvis?" I asked them. "I know he'd appreciate detailed descriptions of those men."

Mrs. Larabee suddenly gasped. "Oh, my! I just thought of something! What if those men did something bad to Mr. Jones? What will happen if they find out we described them to the police?"

Mrs. Bandini managed to look both stern and noble at the same time. "It will keep them from doing terrible things to other people, if we help to catch them."

"Of course," Mrs. Larabee said. "It was just a thought. Someone had to think of it, so I did."

"I'll call Detective Jarvis right now," I said. I got up and turned to walk to the office, but there was Mr. Kamara scurrying toward me.

"Miss . . . Miss Young Lady," he said, and came to a stop right under my nose.

"Mary Elizabeth Rafferty," I said to him.

"Yes. Young lady, you saved my life yesterday."

The way his eyes were drilling into mine made me embarrassed, so I stammered, "That's okay. It wasn't anything." That sounded terrible, so I quickly added, "I mean, I'm glad I could pull you out in time, and I'm sorry you got hurt. But you don't have to thank me."

Then I felt my neck and face turn a hot red, because, of course, he hadn't thanked me.

While I was trying desperately to think of the right thing to say, Mr. Kamara gave a bow and pulled a small box from his pocket, thrusting it at me. "Please accept with my gratitude," he said.

I took a step backward. "Oh, I can't."

"Oh, yes, you can," Mrs. Bandini said.

"At least open the box and see what's in it," Mrs. Larabee said. "It looks like the kind of box they put jewelry in."

"Thank you, Mr. Kamara," I said, "but as an employee of the hotel I should not accept a gift from you."

"Is there a rule?" Mrs. Bandini asked me.

"Well, no," I said, "but it doesn't seem right."

"Is right," Mr. Kamara said.

"After all, you saved his life," Mrs. Larabee said. "You'll hurt his feelings if you don't take his gift."

"Mr. Kamara, your thanks are enough," I said.

"No," he said stubbornly, making little jabbing motions with the box in my direction. "You take."

"I think you are hurting his feelings," Mrs. Bandini said. "You should accept it. Maybe you won't even like it, but what could it hurt you to take it and say thank-you and let the poor man feel better? You can see how upset he is."

That I could see, and I was feeling sorrier for him by the minute. So against my better judgment I reached out for the small box, said, "Thank you, Mr. Kamara," and opened it. Inside, suspended from a thin gold chain, was a gleaming multicolored cloisonné locket about an inch wide and two inches long. "Oh!" I gasped. "It's beautiful!"

Mr. Kamara smiled, but it wasn't a smile of pleasure. It was more a flash of triumph, and it bothered me. Perhaps my expression showed my confusion, because he immediately became more friendly and nodded to Mrs. Bandini and Mrs. Larabee too. "Movie star picture inside," he said with pride, as though he had taken the shot himself.

"Thank you, Mr. Kamara," I said.

He bowed once more, then turned and left the club.

"Let us see!" Mrs. Bandini had a hand out, so I put the box in it.

"A very nice gift," she said. "I've seen these in the hotel gift shop and while, under the circumstances, it would be rude to tell you the price before taxes, you can take my word for it that it didn't cost too much and not too little, so I consider this to be a perfectly respectable gift."

"Put it on," Mrs. Larabee said. "Let's see how it looks."

I took back the small box. "I can't wear jewelry while I'm working," I said.

Mrs. Bandini beamed at me. "It will look lovely when you're all dolled up in a pretty summer dress and going out with a nice tall, good-looking boy—like my grandson Eric. Eric wants to meet you," she added. "I've told him so much about you. In fact, I'm going to bring him to the club this weekend, so the two of you can become acquainted."

I smiled at her over my shoulder as I practically raced back to the office. All I needed was a bigger, meaner version of Pauly at the club.

I unlocked the bottom desk drawer and tucked the little box into my plastic handbag, then locked it up again. The lull would soon be over. Tina would arrive with the new batch of photo-ID cards, and soon afterward the conventioneers would come, wanting to unwind after sitting in straight-backed chairs at meetings all day.

The file box was in front of me, so I decided to go

through the cards and see if any new faces had come in since yesterday. There were just three: a couple who looked happily bemused—yes, their room number showed that they were in the honeymoon suite—and an elderly man whose mouth turned down like an upside-down horseshoe and who peered out from under his bushy eyebrows like a fox from behind a hedge.

His wasn't a new face. That was a face I'd remember, and I was positive that I'd seen it before. I was also positive that this card hadn't been in the file yesterday. When had I seen it? Tuesday? Monday?

I needed to talk to someone, so I called the security office. Tina answered, and I told her about the card that had disappeared and returned.

"If you saw this man's face, would you know if he was one of those who ran into a pickpocket somewhere in Houston?"

"Maybe," Tina said. "What's his name? I'll check the ID file up here."

"Samuel Smith," I read from the card. "Suite 826."

"Got it," Tina said almost immediately.

"Well?"

"If he had any trouble with pickpockets, he didn't report it." Then she said, "That's odd. Let me talk to Lamar. I'll get right back to you."

"What's odd?"

"Lamar's scribbled a little note at the bottom of Smith's card."

"What does it say?"

"I can't decipher it. I think it says, *watch him.*"

"I wonder what it means."

"That's what I'm going to find out. I'll let you know when I bring in the afternoon ID cards."

"Thanks," I said as Tina hung up. I closed the file and

picked up the note with the four circles drawn on it. I
intended to toss it into the wastepaper basket, but I studied it again. There was something about it that nagged at
me. Something familiar.

Fran appeared in the doorway. "Hi," he said.

"Hi," I answered. Fran had the nicest smile.

"The Houston Symphony Orchestra's going to be
playing outdoors in Miller Theater on Sunday. I found
out that's your day off, and I switched with another guy
so I'll be off then too. I'd like to take you to the symphony. We could bring a blanket and some food and sit
on the grass and—"

I didn't hear another word he said. All of a sudden that
crescent of circles made sense. It was like a symphony
orchestra—the string instruments here, the wind instruments there, the drums . . . I jumped to my feet, ran
around the desk, caught the toe of my tennis shoe on the
desk leg, and stumbled into Fran's arms.

"Oh, Fran! You're wonderful! You did it! You did it!"

Fran staggered back but managed to stay on his feet.
He helped me back on mine, looking very pleased with
himself. "I knew that sooner or later I'd come up with
something you'd want to do on a date," he said.

I still held tightly to his shoulders. "No! Listen, Fran.
Listen. It's not the date. It's what you said about the
symphony orchestra. It's those little circles we drew on
the notepad. Don't you see?"

"No," he said. "I don't."

I drew him closer. "Remember? You said that each of
them stood for a separate crime. They weren't related."

He nodded. "Okay. I remember now. But what about
them?"

"They're like the parts of an orchestra, Fran. Each part
is separate, but the conductor brings them together. The

different kinds of crimes that are taking place in the hotel could be tied together, too, if one person were conducting them!"

Fran gaped. "You might be right. But the conductor would have to be someone in the hotel."

I lowered my voice and looked around. "Let's tell Lamar about this."

"We can't do that," Fran said. "The conductor might very well be Lamar."

8

"Oh, not Lamar!" I said.

"Why not?"

"He's so efficient. He cares about his job."

"It could be a front. Who else would know as much about what goes on in the hotel?"

"The manager, Mr. Parmegan."

"Okay. We'll put him on our suspect list too. I can try to keep up with what he's doing each day. He follows a pretty constant routine."

Another thought occurred to me. "Why does the conductor have to be working at the hotel? Why can't he be one of the guests? Mr. Kamara keeps a regular routine, too, and he was the one who knew Mr. Jones."

"Okay. Mr. Kamara's on the list, but I think you're going off in the wrong direction." Fran looked at his watch. "Uh-oh. I've been here long enough. I have to get back."

He stopped at the doorway and turned. "You didn't answer about the symphony tickets. Should I get them?"

"I'm sorry, Fran," I began, but the eager look on his face stopped me. After all, listening to the Houston Symphony Orchestra together wasn't exactly a real date. "I'm sorry I didn't answer you right away," I finished. "Yes. I'd like to go with you."

For a few moments Fran looked as pleased as a puppy when you scratch his tummy. Then he became serious. "I won't see you tonight," he said. "My aunt and uncle are visiting, and my mom made me promise I'd come home as fast as I could, so I could get in on the tail end of the party they're throwing."

"Then I'll see you tomorrow," I said.

"You bet," Fran said, and vanished from the doorway.

I sat at the desk and picked up the sheet of notepad paper. In the center at the bottom, where the conductor would stand, I drew a small box, and inside the box I wrote the letter *K,* for Kamara. Then from that box I drew lines radiating out to each of the circles. Inside circle one I wrote *sofa.* Inside circle two I wrote *meat.* Inside circle three I wrote *stuff,* because naturally there wasn't room to write things like silver and paintings and things like that. Inside circle four I wrote *PP* for pick-pockets.

Now all I had to do was to figure out how Mr. Kamara could manage to orchestrate all these crimes. He'd have to have help. Where would he get it? *Sofa, meat,* and *stuff* left me blank. But on the line to circle four I wrote *Mr. Jones.* What if Mr. Kamara came into the health club office each day when no one was looking, stole some of the cards, gave them to Mr. Jones, who followed the people and stole their wallets? Then, the next day Mr. Jones could bring back the cards and Mr. Kamara could replace them.

There was something wrong with this.

Somebody was almost always in the office or nearby. It would be hard for Mr. Kamara to count on being able to sneak in and out. And this was a large hotel. Lots of types of people stayed at this hotel. How would Mr. Kamara know which ones had wallets worth stealing?

Someone would have to know which guests had lots of money and which didn't. Someone who would see guests opening their wallets, flashing their bills.

Floyd Parmlee? In room service?

I began to get excited. Floyd could tell Mr. Kamara. Mr. Kamara could tell Mr. Jones.

I let out a long sigh. Again I had come to a dead stop. How could Mr. Kamara get the cards in and out of the file box in the health-club office? I'd have to think about that one awhile.

But before I could work on it, two families of petite people came into the office. I recognized the mothers and fathers from their cards. There were half-a-dozen assorted children with the adults. Children rarely showed up on the photo ID's, because—unless their parents were holding them—they were too short to be in range of the hidden camera. No one in the group seemed to understand English, but they understood smiles. I handed them towels and managed to separate them, getting them headed for the appropriate dressing rooms.

The stack of towels on the table near my desk was getting low, so I took more from the closet to add to the pile. Art Mart had apparently stuffed the towels on the closet shelves without any regard for neatness; so I straightened the pile.

"Mary Elizabeth! Where are you?"

The loud hiss in the office startled me. I jumped, dropping some of the towels, and stepped out of the closet.

Mrs. Bandini's eyes were so wide she looked like a little gray-haired owl. "You have got to do something quick!" she said. "The Jacuzzi is filled with naked people!"

I followed her out of the office. The two families who had just come in filled the Jacuzzi. They were chattering and smiling, and bouncing the children from one to another.

They all looked at me. "Do any of you speak English?" I asked.

They just stared.

"Maybe you should call security," Mrs. Bandini said, still in a stage whisper.

"I'll try body language," I said. "Maybe that will do it." So I pointed at Mrs. Bandini, then gave a little tug at the strap of her red bathing suit. "This is a bathing suit," I said.

They looked at each other, then back at me, and laughed as though I'd made a very funny joke. One of the women nodded and gestured at Mrs. Bandini to join them in the Jacuzzi.

So I went through the motion of removing clothes. They watched intently. Then I shook my head and pointed at the Jacuzzi, waiting to see if they understood. They laughed even harder.

I sighed. "I don't know how to make them understand," I said to Mrs. Bandini. "You're right. I'll have to call security."

But the door to the hotel opened, and Lamar came into the room. "Caught it on camera," he said. With his sharply creased authority he stood near the edge of the pool, pointed toward the dressing rooms, and snapped out something in a language that the people in the Jacuzzi understood.

One of the women stood up and said something to him. Lamar nodded as though she'd been speaking in English.

"Towels!" Mrs. Bandini gasped. "Quick! Mary Elizabeth, get these people towels!"

The Jacuzzi people had brought the stack of towels I'd given them. I began handing them out as they stepped up, one by one, out of the Jacuzzi. In a few minutes they had disappeared into the dressing rooms. Mrs. Bandini rushed over to repeat the entire scene to Mrs. Larabee, who hadn't missed a thing.

I turned to Lamar. "I'm impressed! You were able to talk to them!"

Lamar's chin tilted modestly. "All I can say in their language is, 'In this country we have laws against public nudity. You must wear bathing suits in the pool and Jacuzzi.'"

"That's all you can say?"

"This happens every once in a while, so it seemed a good thing to learn."

"But you seemed to understand what that woman said to you."

"Yeah. Someone always says the same thing. I memorized it and got it translated. She said, 'In your country you have some strange laws.'"

"Mr. Boudry," I said, "has Tina talked to you about Mr. Smith?"

"Which Mr. Smith? The hotel always has a lot of Mr. Smiths."

Obviously she hadn't yet. "Mr. Samuel Smith. She said you had written something like *watch him* on his photo-ID card."

"Ah-ha," Lamar said. His eyes became slits, and his mouth pulled into a thin line. "I did. He checked out at noon today."

"Because you watched him?"

He brushed a tiny piece of lint from the front of his suit jacket. "Quite possibly."

"He suspected you knew something about him. Right?"

"I did."

"Look, Mr. Boudry," I said. "This is driving me crazy. What did he suspect that you knew?"

"That the man is syndicate," he said. "Out of Miami."

"How did you know that?"

"I keep in touch," Lamar said. "Besides my network of information, Mr. Smith's picture was in last month's issue of *Crime Facts.*"

"By any chance did Mr. Smith report that his wallet was stolen?"

Lamar's clipped laugh sounded more like a bark. "No. I'm sure that Mr. Smith's wallet was as safe as if it had been in a bank box. No pickpocket would be stupid enough to risk what would happen to him if he stole the wallet of someone high up in a crime syndicate."

I suddenly remembered something and nearly jumped in the air. "Mr. Boudry! Yesterday there were two men in the health club asking about Mr. Jones. When I was downtown at the police station I recognized a picture of one of them. The sergeant told me he was suspected of a tie-in with the Miami syndicate."

Immediately Lamar snapped into a businesslike efficiency, and began to question me. I was glad I had reported the men to Tina. That part seemed to satisfy Lamar.

"If you want a really good description," I said, "ask Mrs. Bandini and Mrs. Larabee." I steered Lamar over to the two women, who puffed up like a pair of pigeons and tried to outtalk each other as Lamar took notes.

The list would soon come in with cards to file and

cards to toss. For some reason I didn't really understand, I took Mr. Samuel Smith's card from the file. Instead of tossing it, because he'd checked out of the hotel, I stuck it under some papers in the back of the bottom drawer of the desk and locked the drawer again.

Groups of people had begun to come to the health club. I checked out the faces in the pool and hurried through the exercise room and women's dressing room, making sure everything was all right. The women and children from the Jacuzzi families had settled into the women's sauna room, still without a stitch of clothing. They laughed and waved at me. I just waved right back and shut the door. At the moment they were the least of my problems.

The evening was busier than the one before. I wished that Art Mart had stuck around. I could have used the help. It wasn't until ten-thirty that the crowd began thinning out.

Once more I walked through the tables on the landing above the inner pool, close to the door to the hotel. I filled a tray with paper cups and napkins, and cola cans, and other rubbish. As I straightened I happened to glance toward the door. A man dressed in a dark business suit was turning away, going back to the hotel. Was he one of the men who had questioned me about Mr. Jones? Two tall, broad baldies in sweatsuits filled the gap in the doorway, and I couldn't see.

I wasn't sure, but I called Lamar anyway.

"I'll check on it," he snapped. The line went dead, and I knew he was halfway down the stairs already. There was nothing to worry about.

It took a few minutes to convince everyone that the health club really did close at eleven P.M., just as the sign on the door said. When the last guests had finally gone it was eleven-ten.

There was still a lot of pickup to do. I managed to collect the towels, which had been draped on chairs, tables, and the tiles near the pool, and dumped them into the overflowing wet towel bin in the women's dressing room. I checked out the sauna, half expecting to see the Jacuzzi people still visiting in there; but the room, of course, was empty. One by one I tidied the shower stalls and the area around the big mirror. I found four more pairs of sunglasses, two cans of hair spray, and a tiny bathing-suit bottom that seemed to match the top I'd found the day before. Finally, I was satisfied by the condition of the women's dressing room, so I went to the door of the men's dressing room and called, "Anybody still here? I'm coming in."

I was pretty sure that no one would be there at this hour. I took a step inside, then stopped. Had I just heard something? I couldn't be sure. For a few seconds I listened intently, not breathing. What was it?

Nothing but my imagination. With a *whoosh* I drew in a deep breath of air and entered the men's dressing room.

I would swear in any court of law that men are a hundred times messier than women at their worst. It took me at least ten minutes just to tidy the room and men's sauna. While I worked I kept muttering, "Who are your maids at the office?" and "Who are your maids at home?" Unfortunately, it wasn't hard to guess the answers. There wasn't anything I could do about it, and right now the maid was *me*. I worked hard and got things ready so that the very-early-morning cleaning crew could step in and make everything shine.

I walked through the exercise room back to the office, grabbed the door frame, and gave a little yelp. Someone had turned off the outside and indoor pool lights. Beyond the office was a well of darkness.

"Who's there?" I whispered. I cleared my throat and tried again. My hands were clammy, and my knees were having trouble holding me up. "Is anybody out there?"

No one answered. There was only silence.

I edged toward the desk, reached down, and dialed the number of the security office. It rang and rang. Finally a voice answered. I didn't recognize it.

"Is Lamar Boudry there?" I asked.

"Nope," he said. "Who is this?"

"Mary Elizabeth Rafferty in the health club. Is Tina there?"

"Nope," he repeated. "What's your problem?"

"The lights are off in the pool area."

"Don't call us. Call maintenance."

"I mean someone turned them off."

"Aren't you supposed to close up anyway by this time?"

I tried not to yell at him. "Where is Lamar?"

"Bar," he said. "Couple of drunks got into a fight."

"Where's Tina?"

"Making rounds. Look, things are extra busy tonight. You got any real problems, call back, but otherwise, don't keep the line busy. Okay?"

"Okay," I mumbled, and hung up.

I stared out the office-window wall into the pool area, but with the light on in the office it was like staring into a black cave. If anyone was out there, I couldn't see him.

So I did what I should have done in the first place, and would have if I hadn't been so scared.

I flipped up every switch on the plate, so that inside and outside the health club was brightly lit.

Carefully I poked my head through the open office

doorway and looked in every direction. Outside the glass wall the trees and shrubbery around the pool shuddered and trembled in a light breeze. A tiny scrap of paper I'd missed skittered across the cement and disappeared under the bushes. But inside the club nothing moved. The plants and trees with their outstretched branches looked like a group of frozen giant-children caught playing statue.

I took a few cautious steps from the office and paused, glancing down into the swimming pool. There, staining the brilliant blue water like a dark spreading ink spot, floated a body.

Even though the body was facedown, I knew who it was. Mr. Kamara.

9

ক

As though my mind were a shark with an open mouth, I gulped in everything at once. Mr. Kamara was dressed in swimming trunks. His robe was neatly draped over the back of a chair near the pool, and his thongs were side by side under the chair, tucked there according to Mr. Kamara's usual tidy habit.

But Mr. Kamara was floating near the surface of the pool, and somebody had to pull him out. At first I had assumed he was dead. How did I know? Maybe he wasn't, and I could save him.

I pulled off my shoes and jumped into the water, so frightened I flailed and thrashed like a novice swimmer. His arms were out, fingers spread and elbows bent. His legs hung lower in the water, so that he looked almost ready to stand—if he could. I swam up behind him, and it took every bit of courage I had to reach out and touch him.

His chin was cold, and I knew as I cupped it in my left hand, pulling it up and out of the water, that I was too late. But I towed him to the shallow water and managed to drag him onto the steps. He lay on his back with water dribbling from one corner of his mouth. His eyes were dark blanks that stared into mine.

Stumbling, crying, I ran to the telephone and screamed at the guard, who answered, "Weren't you watching? Can't you see? He's dead!"

I don't remember what else I yelled, and I have no idea what the man said. But almost by the time I had slammed down the receiver, the door to the hotel flew open and Lamar ran through.

Without a word to me he dashed straight to Mr. Kamara's body and carefully examined it, kneeling on the steps in the water. He shook his head, stood, and looked at me.

"Get a towel for yourself," he said. "And get a handful of Kleenex. Blow your nose."

His voice was so authoritative that I immediately stopped crying and did what he said.

"Now, come here," Lamar called.

I slowly left the office, then stopped. I couldn't go back to the body.

"How did he drown?" Lamar asked.

"I don't know. I didn't even know he was in the pool."

"Do you know how long he was in the water?"

"No!"

"Can you guess?"

I thought hard. "About ten minutes ago I heard a small noise."

"What kind of a noise? Describe it."

"I can't. It was just a . . . noise."

"A splash? Like someone diving?"

"No. I would have recognized a splashing noise."

"Did the noise come from the pool area?"

"I don't even know that, Mr. Boudry. I couldn't place

the sound I'd heard. I was just going into the men's dressing room to put it in order. I waited and listened, but I didn't hear anything else, so I thought it was my imagination."

"How did you get wet?"

"I didn't know Mr. Kamara was dead. I jumped in to try to save him."

"So you didn't find him on the steps like this?"

"No. He was floating in the water." I gave a huge shudder all the way down to my toes, and clutched the towel tightly around me. I took a step sideways and reached out for one of the poolside chairs.

"Don't touch that!" Lamar's words were like a slap.

"But I want to sit down."

"Not there. We want to preserve the scene."

"What are you talking about?" I yelped.

He ignored my question, saying, "Tell me exactly what happened tonight, as far as you know."

I told him quickly, briefly, trying to remember every detail that might be important, as I trembled with the cold and with the fear of what had taken place.

Then, with the pool water still dripping from his trousers and squishing in his shoes, Lamar calmly walked to the office and picked up the telephone. As he waited for someone to answer he looked over his shoulder at me and said—a little more kindly now—"Do you have some dry clothes to change into?"

I nodded, and he snapped, "Then do it. Right now. The police will be here shortly."

"Police?"

But his attention had switched from me to whoever was on the other end of the line.

I put on the dress I had worn to the police station,

towel-dried and brushed my hair, and went back to the pool area to find Lamar, Tina, and two other guards observing a pair of white-shirted paramedics who were bending over Mr. Kamara's body. As I came into the room, everyone but the paramedics turned and stared at me.

I stopped and stared back. I didn't know what to say.

Tina gave her head a little shake, like someone waking from a stupor, and moved toward me. She looked awful. Her throat muscles were jerking as though she were gulping a lot. I'd heard about people turning green. Tina'd really managed to do it. "Oh, Liz!" she said. "This must have been terrible for you."

I couldn't answer. I just shivered.

She put her hands on my shoulders, gave another big gulp, and said, "Lamar told us what you did. You were very brave. You called upon hidden inner resources you didn't even know that you had. Aren't you proud of yourself?"

"No!"

Tina dropped her hands and stepped back. "Well, per- haps the full significance hasn't—"

"I'm not proud of myself," I said. "I should have in- vestigated when I heard the noise. I convinced myself I hadn't heard anything. Maybe if I'd run right out here, I could have saved him from drowning."

"He may not have drowned," Lamar said.

The two paramedics stood up. One moved toward a folding stretcher on wheels, but Lamar stepped into his way. "The police are coming," he said. "Leave the body where it is."

"We haven't got all night," the paramedic said.

"You have if we say you have," Lamar said. Even with

his squishy shoes he was in total command. The guy
shrugged, muttered "Okay," and moved back from the
steps to where his partner was standing.

There was silence for an instant, the way it sometimes
is at parties when everyone stops speaking at once. But it
didn't stay silent for long.

"Pete, make the bar check," Lamar ordered. "Nate,
back on the cameras. No one's in the office, and you're
supposed to be on duty there. Tina"—he paused for just
an instant and glanced in my direction—"Tina, you're
off duty now. You can go home, or you can stick around
for a while."

"I'll stay with Liz," Tina said, getting the message.

"You don't have to," I told her.

"I want to," she answered. She took my hand and led
me to one of the tables away from the pool. Fronds of a
large potted palm provided an interlaced green barrier
between Mr. Kamara's body and us. Liz glanced at the
palm a couple of times as though trying to convince
herself that we couldn't see the steps of the pool. She
huddled back into the web-backed chair and said, "We'll
wait here. By the way, where's your short friend?"

"Fran had to go home as soon as he got off duty. His
family was entertaining visiting relatives."

"Speaking of relatives, have your parents come back
from their trip yet?"

"Not yet."

"Want me to call them?"

I wanted it more than anything I could think of, but I
shook my head. "No. Dad can't interrupt an important
business trip just because . . . because of Mr. Kamara."

"If you're afraid of a guilt trip," she began, but thank-
fully the door from the hotel opened, and two uniformed

police officers came through. They were halfway to the pool when the door opened again and there was Detective Jarvis with another shorter, stockier man who walked the way a policeman walks, with his arms slightly held out from his body. It had to be Detective Jarvis's partner.

He was. Detective Jarvis introduced him to me. Detective Robert Morgan. He nodded at me, then walked over to the body and talked to the paramedics. Jarvis conferred with Lamar, examined Mr. Kamara's body, front and back, and went through the pockets of his robe, coming up empty handed.

Then attention was focused on me. I found myself repeating my story, then repeating it again. As I retold it the third time, I realized that most of the shock had been squeezed from my body by my own words, which came out as sour and dry as brittle, brown bay leaves.

"Was Mr. Kamara in the habit of going swimming after club hours?" Detective Jarvis asked.

"He's never done it since I've worked here," I said.

"I can answer that," Lamar said. "No one is allowed in the pool after closing time, and that includes Mr. Kamara."

"But his robe and thongs are exactly the way he always left them," I said.

Detective Jarvis turned to the paramedics and motioned toward the body. They immediately covered the body, swung it over to the stretcher, and raised it up on its wheels.

"Please take the side door out," Lamar said.

"Yeah, yeah, that's where the dispatcher told us you said to park the vehicle," one of the men drawled. "Don't worry. We won't be going through your lobby."

They didn't seem upset at dealing with a dead body.

Maybe that was so much a part of their job that they got used to it. Or maybe they had learned to cover all the deep, twisting horror and hurt that surely must shiver inside them.

I must have spoken my thoughts aloud as I watched them wheel Mr. Kamara's body out of the health club, because Detective Jarvis, who stood next to me, murmured, "If the day ever comes when I *don't* feel something, I'll quit."

"It's an unhealthy instinct to try to cover one's normal emotions," Tina said. "I was glad to find out you had cried, Liz. *That* was healthy."

Detective Morgan said a few words to Detective Jarvis, then walked out with the paramedics.

Jarvis turned to Lamar. "Thanks for the information and the descriptions of the men whom Mary Elizabeth saw." He nodded toward me. "Those were good, clear, helpful descriptions."

"They weren't my descriptions," I told him. "A couple of women who were in the club gave Mr. Boudry those descriptions."

"They took in a lot of detail. Tell them I said, good work."

"They'll like that," I answered. I looked at Lamar. "Could I go home now?"

"In just a moment," he said, "as soon as you give us Mr. Kamara's locker number." Lamar turned to Detective Jarvis. "You'll want to look in his locker, won't you?"

"Yes," Detective Jarvis said. "Any need for a warrant?"

"No," Lamar said, "because the lockers are the property of the health club, which is the property of the hotel. Anyone using a locker is using it courtesy of the hotel."

Detective Jarvis nodded. "Same setup for his room."

"Right."

"Might as well get with it."

They both looked at me. "There's a book in the top drawer with the locker assignments in it," I said. "I'll get Mr. Kamara's number for you." I took two steps toward the office, then turned back to them. "Why are you doing all this investigating? Just because he drowned?"

"We're not sure that he drowned," Detective Jarvis said. "We'll get the facts from the medical examiner tomorrow."

They looked at each other as though they both knew something the rest of us didn't know.

"Why aren't you sure?" I asked.

"Because," Detective Jarvis said, "Mr. Boudry and I noticed a slight depression on the back of Mr. Kamara's head. Maybe he slipped and bumped his head as he fell into the pool, or maybe . . ."

He stopped, and Lamar finished the sentence, "Or maybe somebody else put that bruise there."

"Murder?" Tina's voice was overloud and echoed through the room.

Lamar shrugged and said, "If Mary Elizabeth will get Kamara's locker number for us . . ."

I got it in a hurry. I also got the spare key for the lock and led the way to the end of the men's locker room. It was the last locker on the top row. I stood back while Detective Jarvis opened the locker.

But all the time I was doing this I was reliving what had happened. I could see myself flooding the area with light, discovering Mr. Kamara's body, and pulling it to the steps. His blank eyes kept staring into mine. I had never seen a dead person. I felt sick to my stomach and wished I could wake up and find this had never happened.

There wasn't much in the locker. A short-sleeved sport shirt, one rubber thong, and a half-empty bottle of expensive men's cologne.

"It doesn't tell us much," Detective Jarvis said.

"It does in a way," I said.

"How do you mean?"

"Something's missing. The wallet. Mr. Kamara's wallet and room key should be in the locker. People from the hotel usually get locks for their lockers and put their wallets and room keys in them. People rarely leave wallets in their hotel rooms. Mr. Kamara never did."

"Good point," Tina said. She tried to smile at me and didn't quite make it. In spite of being older and working in security, it was obvious that she felt as miserable as I did.

"It's a very good point," Detective Jarvis said. He made a notation in his notebook.

"This whole thing is weird," I said. "You didn't find his wallet or room key in his robe pockets, did you? And they aren't here. He wouldn't have left his room without both of them—especially the key. He'd need the key to get back into his room."

"So it really was murder," Tina whispered. One corner of her mouth twisted down and she choked out, "Excuse me. I'm going to the ladies' room." She turned and ran.

"Should I go with her?" I asked Jarvis.

"She'll be all right," he said. "How about you? You don't look any better than she did."

I backed up and sat on one of the wooden benches that stretched down the middle of the dressing room. I took a couple of deep breaths. It didn't help. In spite of the air conditioning that circulated the air through the club, the dressing room still stank of wet feet and deodorant soap and dirty, wet towels. And Mr. Kamara's dark eyes were still staring into mine.

"Real murder's not like a murder in a Chevy Chase movie," I said.

"No, it's not," Detective Jarvis answered.

"Excuse me," I said. "I think—" I bolted after Tina.

A few minutes later, as we splashed cold water on our faces, Tina said, "It's a normal reaction for the mind and the body to cooperate in rejecting that which they do not want to accept."

"Oh, come on, Tina," I said, mopping up my face with a clean towel, "why can't you just face it that we threw up?"

For a moment I thought she was going to cry. "An efficient security guard should be in total control at all times."

"Only Lamar," I said. "He's one of a kind." I took her shoulders and smiled at her. "Hey, you're a nice, normal person, and you reacted the way a nice, normal person would. Remember what Detective Jarvis said? That if he didn't feel something he'd quit?"

"I guess," Tina said. She pushed a strand of hair back from her face and stared at me in the mirror. "I'm not going to be a security guard forever. I'm going to work hard and get my degree. And I'm not going to be just any old average psychologist either. I'm going to write books to help people and become rich and famous. You'll see me on TV."

"I'll watch for you."

She attempted to smile, and the corners of her mouth

quivered. "When I start my practice, how would you like to be my assistant?"

"You'd lose your patients," I said. "You'll need a serene assistant, not someone who drops things and falls over coffee tables."

"Basically," she said, "awkwardness comes from your mind not being willing to adjust quickly to rapid body growth, which comes right down to a bottom line of insecurity. You need a stronger self-image. Have you thought about—"

"Let's go, Tina." I tugged at her hand. "If Detective Jarvis doesn't need us any longer, I want to go home."

He and Lamar were in the health-club office. Jarvis gave Tina and me a quick glance. "Anything else you can think of to tell me? Anything else you know that Mr. Kamara had or did?"

"No," I said.

"Thanks for staying," he said. "You can go home now."

I squeezed around him and sat at the desk. I unlocked the bottom drawer and removed my purse, locked it again, and dropped the key into its place in the top, middle desk drawer.

"Let us know what you find out," I said.

"We will," Jarvis said.

It was past midnight. At this time no one was at the employee check-out station, so Tina and I quickly went through and to our cars. She waved at me as she drove off.

Even with the bright arc lights in the parking lot it was lonely and scary. I fumbled with numb fingers, trying to start Old Junk Bucket, and gave a yelp of relief when his motor finally took hold.

It wasn't until I was safely home, inside the house, my back against the locked door and the living-room lights on, that I could begin to let go. I shivered, wrapping my arms around myself, and allowed myself to cry.

I fished inside my plastic purse for a tissue, but my fingers bumped the small box that held the cloisonné locket. I took out the box, opened it, and examined the locket as it winked and glimmered in the lamplight.

It was strange, too, the way Mr. Kamara had given me the locket with such a peculiar delight. I wondered. Should I have told Detective Jarvis about this locket?

10

I promised myself to sleep late the next morning. Promises about sleeping late aren't any good if you don't spread the word around to people who could help you keep them.

Mom called.

"Mmmmph," I breathed into the telephone, trying to untangle my legs from the sheet and keep from falling out of bed at the same time.

"What are you doing, sweetheart?" Mom asked.

"Sleeping," I managed to grunt.

"At this hour?" Mom's voice rose in surprise. "Why, it's after ten-thirty! Almost twenty to eleven! Are you feeling all right?"

"Sleepy," I said.

"Goodness," Mom said, "you're wasting the best part of the day."

"Morning people always say irritating things like that," I told her, and giggled, because I sounded like Tina and her pop psychology.

Mom giggled too. "I'll let you get back to sleep," she said, "if you tell me one thing. How are you? Is everything all right? The dishwasher isn't acting up again, is it? Do you need anything?"

"That's more than one thing, and everything's fine," I said.

Mom sighed. "You're a young woman now, Liz. I shouldn't worry about you. Your father says to me over and over, 'Nothing's going to happen to Liz. She's fine.' "

"I'm fine," I said.

"Are you eating properly?"

"Mom!" I was more awake now. "You promised you wouldn't ask me that."

"Well, I just don't want you living on junk food. I bought all those nice vegetables and that big bag of Golden Delicious apples. You love apples, I know. You are enjoying the apples, aren't you?"

"Constantly," I said. "I slice them on my pizza."

"Mary Elizabeth," Mom said, "I love you, and I miss you. Take good care of yourself."

"I will until you get home, Mom, and then I'll give up and let you do it," I said.

She laughed. "Your father sends his love too."

"I love you both," I said. "Good-bye, Mom."

"Good-bye, sweetheart," she said, and we hung up together.

For a moment I snuggled back into the blanket, feeling cosy and warm from both the blanket and from Mom's voice. But I was awake enough now to remember, and the remembrance of last night was like a cold bucket of water dumped on my head.

I couldn't stay in bed another moment. I washed my hair, rubbed some mousse into it, and set it on hot rollers. Then I put some green stuff on my nose and chin. It looked kind of sickening, but I'd bought it after reading that it banished zits forever. I pulled on my old jeans and my favorite T-shirt printed with NOBODY'S PERFECT and went into the kitchen to make breakfast.

The open refrigerator was yawning at me when the doorbell rang. I knew who that would be. Mrs. Zellendorf. I had got in awfully late last night, and I bet she knew all about it. How can you be independent and at the same time have a next-door neighbor checking on you?

In my bare feet I padded down the hall to the front door and threw it wide open. There stood Fran. He was holding a sack of doughnuts.

He blinked, then smiled. "You're a walking advertisement for your T-shirt," he said.

"I thought you were Mrs. Zellendorf."

"Do we look alike?"

"No. But—"

"If I were Mrs. Zellendorf, would you invite me in?"

"Well, sure, but—"

"Hi," he said. "I'm Mrs. Zellendorf."

I had to giggle. "Come in, Fran. Go straight back to the kitchen. Just excuse me for a moment."

"Don't change on my account," he said. "You look good to me even with that sickening guck on your face."

I washed my face, put on a little bit of blusher and blue eye shadow, and combed out my hair. "Why?" I asked my reflection, peering nose to nose in the mirror. "Why do you care? It's just Fran."

The mirror didn't say a word, so I joined Fran in the kitchen. He had already poured two glasses of milk and put the sack of doughnuts on the table.

"Where do you keep the paper napkins?" he asked.

I got the napkins and plates, sat across from him, and fished out a jelly doughnut.

"I had to get out of the house," Fran said, his mouth

full of doughnut. "My uncle's six feet five, and he intimidates me."

"I can't imagine anyone intimidating you." I took a big bite, and the tart raspberry jelly exploded into my mouth.

"Uncle Ralph does, but he proves my theory. I asked him how he did in school, and he said okay. Just okay. I asked if he worried about being only okay, and he said it didn't bother him at all, because he spent most of his time playing first string on the football team. See what I mean? No stress, no worries, and he gets to be six feet five."

"Then why don't you just stop worrying about school?" I asked.

"It may be too late," he said glumly. He licked his fingers and added, "Either your nose is bleeding, or you missed with the jelly in your doughnut."

I wiped off my nose and pulled a second doughnut from the bag. Fran did too.

He took another bite and said, "I thought about you last night. I hoped you wouldn't be afraid, and I wished I could be with you. I missed you. So—how did it go?"

I dropped my doughnut and burst into tears.

In an instant Fran was beside me, his arms around me. He kept murmuring little snuggly things into my neck. "You missed me too, huh? It's okay. I'm here now. Don't cry."

I pulled back, grabbed my napkin, which was gritty with granulated sugar, wiped my eyes, and blew my nose. "I'm not crying about you, Fran," I said. "Sit down, and I'll tell you what happened."

As I recounted the story, Fran leaned forward with interest. "There goes your theory about Mr. Kamara being the one who orchestrated all the crimes."

"Not necessarily," I said. "Maybe that's why he was killed."

"By whom?"

"I'm not sure."

"And why?"

"There are a few things about this case I don't know yet," I said.

"Like everything," Fran said.

"Don't rub it in."

"Why don't you just forget all about the problem and let your detective friend take care of it?"

I thought a moment. "Maybe it's because of my job. I'm supposed to be responsible for the well-being of the guests of the health club. Maybe I feel guilty because I didn't investigate that noise I heard last night. Maybe it's because I'm scared, and I want the police to catch the murderer as soon as they can." I rubbed my nose with the back of one hand. The sugar felt scratchy.

"I have a good idea," Fran said. "Let's go to the zoo, and eat hot dogs, and ride on the Hermann Park train, and forget all about the Ridley Hotel until it's time to go to work."

My immediate reaction was to say no. But getting away from the problem for a little while made sense. I pushed my chair back from the table. "Okay. Let's go."

"Wash your face first," Fran said. "If you go out like that, you'll attract bees."

I did, and pulled a clean health-club T-shirt and shorts from the drier, stuffing them into a paper bag.

"We can take my car and go from the zoo to the hotel, and I'll take you home when our shifts are over," Fran said. So I got my plastic purse from where I had left it on the hall table. I took the small box from it and laid it on the table, following Fran out the front door and to his car.

Fran's car made Old Junk Bucket look good. As he put his key in the ignition, he patted what was left of the dashboard and said, "Come on, Yellow Belly. Don't let me down."

With a wheeze and rattle the car started. Nervously, we headed for the Hermann Park Zoo.

Fran had been right. Going to the zoo was a good idea. We had a wonderful time and made it back to the Ridley not only on time, but a little early. My watch said two-forty P.M.

As I entered the club from the hotel, Mrs. Bandini and Mrs. Larabee sat bolt upright. They were seated where they could watch the door and catch me when I came in. They both waved and motioned to me, but I pretended that I didn't understand what they wanted. I just smiled and waved back and hurried into the office.

Deeley Johnson was behind the desk. Deeley was trim, compact, and perky, with a big smile for everyone who came into the club. Her hair was no longer than an inch anywhere on her head, and on her it looked great. "Hey, girl!" she said. "Did you think I was never coming back?"

"I'm sorry you were sick," I said.

"No big deal. I'm just sorry I missed all the excitement."

Mr. Kamara's staring black eyes suddenly popped into my mind, and I shuddered. "It wasn't exciting, Deeley. It was horrible."

"Yeah," she said. "I guess it was."

"I'm glad you're back," I told her.

"So's Art Mart. He told me he was going to sleep till noon today. Too bad he didn't get the chance."

"Why didn't he?"

Her eyes widened. "That's right. You didn't hear about the break-in."

"Where? What break-in?"

"Let me tell you. Two of them, in fact. When the police went up to Mr. Kamara's suite, after you went home last night, they found it had been gone over. Stuff was all over the floor and thrown out of the closet. I mean, it was a real mess."

"Somebody must have been looking for something."

"Down here too. Whoever it was did a job on the health club. All the drawers in the desk were open—they broke the lock on the bottom drawer—and nothing was left on the closet shelves."

"What did they take?"

"Nobody knows," she said. "Art Mart couldn't find anything missing."

I gasped as it occurred to me. "If they came back after I had locked up, how did they get in?"

"Good question," she said. "The door between the hotel and the club was locked up tight."

"Deeley!" I said. "The wall!"

She looked puzzled, and I realized that she wouldn't know, so I told her about the gap in the wall.

"Did Lamar or Art tell Detective Jarvis about the wall?" I asked.

"Probably," she said.

"Where is Art?"

"Gone home for a while. He's in a real grouchy mood."

"I suppose he didn't like having to put back everything in the closet."

Deeley stood and stretched. Then she laughed. "Are you kidding? Do you really think that Art Mart would do all that work with me here?"

We grinned at each other.

"This has been a bad morning," she said. "The pool company came and drained the pool, and scrubbed it down, and now they're practically through filling it up again. Nobody's supposed to go in today, because it's going to take till tomorrow to get the water heated properly."

"But I saw a number of people here in the club."

"Some of them only want to sunbathe or use the exercise equipment. Oh. And it's okay if they want to use the Jacuzzi." She glanced out the window at Mrs. Bandini and Mrs. Larabee and lowered her voice. "Some of them just want to talk. Watch out for those two."

The card file was near her elbow. Now was a good time to bring it up. I told her about some of the cards missing, then returning to the file. "Have you ever noticed that?" I asked.

She thought a moment, then shrugged. "I never paid that much attention. An awful lot of people come and go through the hotel. Anyhow, why would some of the cards be missing? What would it mean?"

"I don't know yet," I said.

"Probably every now and then a card gets accidentally misplaced."

"Maybe."

Deeley pointedly glanced at the clock. "I'll keep the desk till you get changed," she said.

Two minutes to three. I hurried into the women's dressing room. I locked my purse inside my locker, since the desk lock was broken, and soon returned to the office dressed in the health-club uniform.

"Hope your day's better than yesterday," Deeley said. "See you tomorrow." She quickly left the club.

Plopping into the desk chair, I suddenly remembered

Mr. Smith's card. I opened the bottom drawer and picked up the few papers that were lying scrambled on the bottom, thumbing through them. The card was gone.

I methodically went through every drawer in the desk. There weren't that many papers in it. A few notes about things that probably should have been thrown away a long time ago, out-of-date fliers about health runs, and things like that, but no sign of Mr. Smith's card. Obviously someone had taken it.

Maybe Art or Deeley or whoever had cleaned the desk had tossed it. I went through the wastepaper basket. Obviously it hadn't been emptied since the nightly cleanup crew had been here, because it was full of Deeley's candy and gum wrappers and Art Mart's diet drink cans. The card wasn't in the basket either.

Why would someone want that card? Is that what the ransacker had been looking for? Surely not. It could have been taken out of the file at any time. Then where was the card?

I glanced through the window to the pool to see Mrs. Bandini and Mrs. Larabee pointedly staring at me, so I strolled over to join them.

"Sit down, sit down," Mrs. Bandini said as she patted a chair that had been deliberately arranged between the two women.

I did.

"Tell us what happened last night," Mrs. Larabee said.

First, I repeated what Detective Jarvis had said about their description of the two men in business suits. They were so pleased with themselves that their cheeks turned pink.

"Next time your son-in-law tells you you're nosy, you can tell him it's a talent that can come in handy," Mrs. Larabee said to Mrs. Bandini.

"His word was *curious,* not *nosy,*" Mrs. Bandini said.

"A matter of semantics," Mrs. Larabee said. She turned to me. "Tell us everything that happened, Mary Elizabeth. We heard you were once more a heroine."

"Heroine? No." Unshed tears swelled painfully behind my eyes. I didn't want to cry again, so as quickly as I could I told the women everything I could remember about what had happened the night before.

As I ended the story, my appreciative audience burst into a duet of clucks and sighs and hum-humming.

"Was it murder or not?" Mrs. Bandini asked.

"I guess no one will know until the medical examiner gives his report."

Mrs. Larabee laid a plump hand on my arm. "When you find out, tell us."

I shifted in the chair. My legs were getting cramped. This was a good time to end the conversation, so I stood and stretched. "I will," I said.

"I beg your pardon. Can you help me?"

The voice was behind us. The three of us turned in one motion, as though we were on a string. A blond woman, who was probably in her early forties, looked at me inquisitively.

"I saw your T-shirt," she said. "No one else was in the office. Could you help me?"

"Of course," I said, and tripped over the chair leg in my rush to assist her.

She held out a hand to steady me. She wasn't a beautiful woman, but she was attractive. Her hair was tightly pulled back into a knot at her neck. She had on a little too much makeup, but I recognized her cream silk jacket and skirt from one of the fashion magazines. Expensive. So was her gold jewelry. Her pale leather handbag hung on her arm, the clasp ajar, her sunglasses hooked over the side.

Mrs. Bandini and Mrs. Larabee were initially impressed. I could tell from the quality of their silence as they waited to hear what she would say.

"My name is Mrs. Kasha Vendra," she said. "I'm Mr. Asmir Kamara's sister."

"Oh!" I said. "I'm terribly sorry about what happened to Mr. Kamara."

"Yes," she said. Her eyelids slowly lowered like smudged blue window shades before she once again raised her glance to meet mine. "A terrible accident."

Mrs. Bandini struggled out of her chair. "I'm Sylvia Bandini," she said, "and this is my friend, Olga Larabee. You have our condolences."

Mrs. Vendra barely nodded in Mrs. Bandini's direction. She didn't even look at her. "Will you please allow me to take the contents of my brother's locker?" she asked me.

"I'll have to get permission," I said.

"That's ridiculous!"

I tried to ease the situation and smiled. "It won't take long. I'll call the security chief right away."

"No!" She took a deep breath. By the time she had exhaled it, she was once more under control. "I'm sorry," she said. "This whole situation is very upsetting."

"Of course," Mrs. Bandini said. She moved nearer. "You and your brother were probably very close friends, as a brother and sister should be, even though he must have been much older than you."

Mrs. Vendra ignored Mrs. Bandini. "I am his only relative," she told me. "Naturally, I will inherit everything. The money—well, there's a lot of it, but it doesn't matter. What matters are Asmir's personal things, the items of sentimental value. Do you understand?"

"Of course," I said.

"So if I could just see what was in his locker?"

"Come with me," Mrs. Bandini said to her. "We'll find a nice place to sit and chat while Mary Elizabeth calls security." Without giving Mrs. Vendra a chance to answer, Mrs. Bandini practically barged into her, grabbing her arm and causing her handbag to fall. Since it was already open the contents spilled across the tiles.

"Oh, my! How clumsy of me!" Mrs. Bandini dropped to her knees and began scooping sunglasses and lipstick and wallet and keys back into Mrs. Vendra's handbag, while Mrs. Vendra fumed.

I had to help Mrs. Bandini to her feet by tugging on the arm she waved in my direction. She gave Mrs. Vendra her handbag, still babbling apologies.

"Later," Mrs. Vendra said to me as she snatched her bag from Mrs. Bandini and tucked it under her arm. "I am totally unnerved. This is all too much for me."

She turned and swept from the club.

"Call security," Mrs. Bandini said to me.

"But she's left."

"Call them anyway. Right away. Tell them a blond hussy type woman was here posing as Mr. Kamara's sister."

"I can't do that. How do you know she isn't his sister?"

"Intuition, for one thing," she said, "and for another the name in her wallet. It wasn't Mrs. Kasha Vendra."

11

I ran to the telephone in the health-club office, Mrs. Bandini and Mrs. Larabee scurrying after me. I called the security office, and told the guard who answered what Mrs. Bandini had said.

Lamar came into the club a short time later and told me they had found no sign of the woman in the hotel.

"Nate was monitoring the cameras in the office, but he wasn't concerned about what was going on in the health club, so he didn't pay attention to the woman. Can you describe her?" he asked as he pulled out a notebook and pen.

"Sure," I said. "Expensive."

Lamar sighed. "Meaning?"

"Great clothes. Silk jacket and skirt, and chunked up with lots of gold jewelry. Her face was kind of middle aged, but her hair was younger."

I paused, and he said, "Hair was younger?"

"Light blond. I can't think of anything else."

Mrs. Bandini subtly slid in front of me. "The woman was wearing a Liz Claiborne outfit, cream-colored silk. Costly, but not too costly. I have a Liz Claiborne blouse myself. She was about five feet six, but she was wearing three-inch heels. Beige lizard shoes and matching handbag. I didn't catch the label on the handbag. She was in her forties, but I recognize a good face-lift when I see it. She wasn't a natural blonde by any means. I know the shade. It's called 'golden ash,' and her hair was pulled back into a French knot. Not many women wear a French knot any longer, so I think she did her hair that way just for this occasion."

Mrs. Bandini ran out of breath, so Mrs. Larabee picked up the string of words and ran with it. "Her jewelry wasn't all real gold. The bracelet was. It had inscriptions on it—sort of like Egyptian hieroglyphics—and the chain could have been."

"Maybe yes, maybe no," Mrs. Bandini said. "Although I prefer no."

"I'm telling this now," Mrs. Larabee said to her friend.

Mrs. Bandini shrugged and let Mrs. Larabee continue.

"The earrings were definitely not," Mrs. Larabee said. "They were costume jewelry and a little too large for her face."

"Decidedly," Mrs. Bandini said.

Lamar's pen had been wildly dashing across his notepad. Now he looked up at the three of us.

"Anything else?"

"Blue eyes," Mrs. Bandini said. "There is no way she could have been Mr. Kamara's sister. And there was no way she was Mrs. Kasha Vendra, as she said she was, when the name on her driver's license was Lily Payne."

Lamar made a final notation, then tucked his pad and pen back into his inside coat pocket. I got a quick glimpse of his shoulder holster and gun. "Thank you for an excellent job of description," he said.

Mrs. Larabee playfully poked Mrs. Bandini in the ribs

with her elbow. They giggled. "The detective also thinks we're pretty good at describing people," she said. "Maybe we should go to work for the Houston police."

"If this woman comes back—" Lamar said to me.

I finished his sentence. "I'll call you immediately."

As he turned to leave the office I said, "Mr. Boudry, have you been in touch with Detective Jarvis? Has he told you yet what the medical examiner said about Mr. Kamara?"

Lamar's shoulders squared professionally. "I was right," he said. "Death was caused by a strong blow to the head. Mr. Kamara didn't drown. He was dead before he hit the water."

"Could he . . ." I didn't want to face it. "Could he have slipped and fallen?"

"Mr. Kamara was murdered," Lamar said. He strode out of the office.

Mrs. Bandini and Mrs. Larabee wanted to talk, but I didn't want to listen. Somehow I managed to herd them back to their chairs by the pool, and returned to the office. I had assumed that, with the pool closed for the day, everything at the club would be pretty quiet, but people kept wandering in to ask questions and stare at the pool as though an outline of the body would be marking the surface of the water. Fortunately for me, Mrs. Bandini and Mrs. Larabee were delighted to answer everyone's questions. They had lunch by the pool and held court even through their chicken almond salad on egg twist rolls.

Eventually they had to go home and make dinner. I made a sign and taped it to the door to the club, so the usual evening crowd would know in advance that the pool was closed, and that helped. Only an occasional guest wandered in to use the exercise equipment or

Jacuzzi. The photo-ID cards were brought and filed, and Art Mart showed up briefly around seven-thirty.

"Your sign looks tacky," he said.

"I didn't have time to go to a printer's. Besides, it's doing the job."

"Anything new around here?"

"Like what?"

"How do I know like what? That's what I asked you."

"Well, Mr. Boudry said it was definite that Mr. Kamara was murdered. He was hit on the head. He didn't drown."

"Maybe he fell and hit his head."

"That's what I suggested, but Mr. Boudry said no."

"They don't know everything."

I told Art about the woman who said she was Mr. Kamara's sister. He frowned the entire time I told him and muttered something under his breath. "Nobody tells me anything!" he grumbled. "And I'm in charge of this club!" He moved closer to me and scowled right into my face. I could smell the sweet-sour pungency of his exotic and cheap shaving lotion. It was all I could do to keep from holding my nose.

I said, "If you were here more, you'd *see* what was going on."

"I don't get paid for overtime!" he snapped. He walked toward the office door.

"Where are you going?" I asked him.

"Home," he said. "This place is dead."

"Don't you want to stick around for a while?"

But he had already disappeared. In a minute I heard the big door to the hotel slam closed.

It was only nine fifty-five when the last guest left. The club was bright with light but echoed with a hollow emptiness. Occasionally there was a creak or snap or pop, as though someone were in the club. I'd jump to my feet and edge toward the sound, but nothing would be there. I strolled through the women's dressing room, almost hoping there would be towels to pick up, but—aside from an open tube of suntan lotion that soured the air— the room was tidy. The hands of the wall clock moved so slowly that I wished I could climb up and help them along.

Finally it was ten forty-five, and I sighed with relief. I'd take care of the men's dressing room now and be ready to leave the moment that Fran showed up.

Automatically, I went to the door of the dressing room and called out, "Anyone here? I'm coming in."

There was no answer, so I made my check. The few men who had been in here had done what they could to make up for their missing brothers. There was soap on the floor, wrappers tossed on the bench, dirty towels lying where they had been dropped, and a spilled bottle of shampoo that spread out of one of the showers all over the tiled floor.

I took care of some of the mess. The custodians could finish the job when they arrived.

Last on my list was the sauna. I opened the door wide and was met by a blast of steam in my face. Someone must have walked away and left this thing on. But there was a timer that regulated the steam and that had to have been set less than forty minutes ago. I turned on the light in the sauna, wondering why it had been turned off.

A body rose up from the wooden benches.

I screamed.

It leapt upward, shouting, and threw a towel at me.

As fast as I could I slammed the sauna door and raced to the telephone to call security, colliding with Fran as I skidded around the doorway into the office. Together we fell across the desk.

He grunted a bit as I reached over him and dialed the number for the security office.

"Somebody get here fast! I need help!" I yelled, and dropped the receiver.

"I'll help if you let me get up," Fran said.

I rolled off him, landing on the floor. He managed to climb off the desk and pick me up.

"Watch out!" I said, so scared I was stuttering. "There's a naked crazy person in the men's sauna!"

"Take it easy," Fran said. "If he comes this way I'll protect you." He dashed into the exercise room, grabbed a five-pound dumbbell, and cautiously edged toward the door to the men's dressing room. "Nobody's in here," he called out.

The door leading to the hotel burst open. I could hear heavy footsteps thunder across the tiles. By the time I had moved out from behind the desk, Lamar and Pete skidded into the office.

"What is it?" Lamar asked.

"There's a crazy man in there." I pointed toward the men's dressing room.

In a minute I heard Fran yelp. "It's not me!"

I ran toward the dressing room, where Pete had Fran in a hammerlock, and Lamar was holding the dumbbell. "No!" I shouted. "That's Fran. He works in room service. The crazy man is in the sauna."

Pete dropped Fran as he and Lamar loped to the sauna and tore open the door.

"You could have been more explicit," Fran complained as he rubbed his neck and tucked his shirt back into his jeans.

"I'm sorry," I said. "This place has me unnerved."

"Put this towel around him," I heard Lamar say.

He and Pete emerged from the sauna supporting a skinny, woebegone, sagging guy whose legs looked as though the bones had dissolved and run out of his toes. A towel was tied around his hips.

"What kind of hotel is this?" the man said. His thin hair hung over his eyes.

"Why were you hiding in there?" Lamar asked him.

"I wasn't hiding," the man said. "I was trying to sweat out a cold." He gave a loud sniffle.

"The club was closed."

"How would I know that? I fell asleep." He gave a huge sniffle, tilting back his head. "I need to blow my nose."

Lamar and Pete let go of his arms. He snatched off the towel he was wearing and loudly blew his nose on it, as I turned and raced out of the room.

Fran joined me in the office. "There are hazards in your job," he said. "Let me take you away from all this."

"As soon as the others leave. I have to lock up."

"They'll be out in a minute. Are you ready?"

"I'll get my handbag."

I unlocked my locker and took out my plastic purse, leaving my jeans and shirt hanging there. The way things had been going it wouldn't hurt to have an extra outfit on hand. I went back to the office through the health club just as Lamar, Pete, and the wretched-looking guy came through the door on the men's side. He was dressed now, his room key dangling in one hand, one of the club's tissue boxes in the other.

The man squinted at Fran, then scowled. "You're room service. I remember you."

"I remember you too," Fran said. "Three hot rum toddies."

"Bring me another one."

"Tomorrow," Fran said. "I'm off duty now."

"This is a rotten hotel," the man said.

"We'll escort you to your room, sir," Lamar said. He and Pete briskly walked on, the man stumbling between them, trying to keep up.

I turned off all the lights, locked the office door, and gripped Fran's hand as we sprinted toward the exit. With great relief I stood in the hotel's hallway and locked the door to the club.

We went through the employee check-out, the elderly guard at the door routinely searching my already see-through purse, and out into the parking lot.

A car was parked next to the trash containers, its passenger door wide open. I grabbed Fran's arm to stop him and put a finger over his lips.

He nibbled it.

"Stop that," I hissed. "Be quiet!"

"What's the matter?" he whispered.

"Shhhh. Follow me." Staying as close to the building as I could to remain out of the glare of the arc lights, and walking silently on the grass, I edged toward the side of the trash bins and peeked around them. There was the man I had seen at the bins before—one of the assistant chefs. He was rummaging through the garbage in the nearest container.

Fran leaned around me, his face pressed against my shoulder.

Finally the assistant chef grabbed something and pulled it free. He hopped down and brushed what looked like carrot and potato peelings off the package. It was about two feet long and a foot thick and well wrapped in plastic, which shone under the arc lights. He tossed the package into his car. I heard it thump against something else. Probably another package.

He slammed the car door and walked around the front of his car. I pulled Fran back into the shadows, as the assistant chef started his car and turned on his headlights.

After he drove off I leaned against Fran and started to laugh.

"What's so funny?" he asked. "Some people might get a big laugh out of a guy putting garbage in his car, but personally I feel that—"

"Fran," I interrupted. "Do you know what we saw?"

"A guy putting garbage in his car. I just said so."

"No," I said. "We just saw the woodwind section drop out of the orchestra."

He put a hand on my forehead. "You don't have a fever. Do you feel delirious?"

"Don't you remember? We talked about each crime being orchestrated. One of the crimes was stealing meat from the kitchens."

"Go on."

"That's what we were watching. That guy is one of the assistant chefs. And I'd bet what we saw was a well-wrapped standing rib roast. Don't you see? He wraps the cuts of meat he wants in plastic and puts it in the garbage containers. Then he pulls them out of the garbage at night and makes off with them. He doesn't have to worry about getting the meat out of the building under Lamar's scrutiny. Some innocent person who is emptying the garbage from the kitchens is carrying the roasts out for him, and he—or someone else—is selling them below market cost to the manager of some second-rate restaurant who doesn't ask questions."

Fran sounded impressed. "If that's true, you solved part of the case!"

"Let's go back and tell Lamar."

"It's too late for him to catch up with the guy."

"He can keep a watch on him and catch him next time."

"Why don't we tell Lamar tomorrow?" Fran said. "I thought I could take you home and we could play some records and have some soft drinks and—"

"No," I said. "It's late. We'll tell Lamar now."

Fran grumbled, but he walked back with me to the employee entrance. Luckily, Lamar was there, saying good-night to the guard, who passed us as we opened the door. I told Lamar what we had seen.

Lamar's eyes became glittery slits again, and his shoulders rose and squared themselves. It was impressive.

"Excellent work," he said when I finished the story. "You say you recognized this man. Do you know his name?"

"No," I said.

"Then give me a description." He pulled out his notepad and pen.

"Okay," I said, and scrunched up my forehead, trying to think of the right words. "He's medium height, average kind of face. He was kind of grungy—especially after he'd gone through the garbage. Really a yucky type. Put down 'yucky.'"

I paused, and Lamar sighed. "That's it?"

"Uh—I think his hair is dark. And so is his moustache. At least they look dark in the parking lot. However, those lights are weird. They make lipstick look purple."

Lamar looked at Fran. "Can you add anything to that description?"

"His name," Fran said. "It's Marco Soledat. I see the guy in the kitchen every day."

Lamar and I just stared at Fran. "Why didn't you say so right away?" I asked him.

"I didn't want to interrupt you," he said. "I was enjoying your description. That was the worst job of description I ever heard."

"Thanks to both of you," Lamar said. He glanced quickly from side to side and lowered his voice. "Just keep this whole thing quiet. Catching Soledat in the act will depend on your not saying another word about it—even to each other."

"Right," Fran said. He clicked his heels together.

"Right," I echoed.

Fran pivoted on one heel, took my arm, and pulled me out to the parking lot.

"I'm hungry," Fran said.

I thought about what we had in the refrigerator. "Would you like an apple?"

He grinned. "Did you happen to get it from a snake?"

I gazed into space, which—of course—was over Fran's head, and sighed. "Be practical," I said.

Fran looked a little hurt. I didn't want to hurt him. But before I could think of what to say that might help, he said, "Let's hope Yellow Belly starts," and led me toward his car.

It was a short ride from the hotel. Fran chatted about stuff at school, and before long the embarrassment between us had dissolved like fog under a Houston sun.

I unlocked our front door and flipped on a couple of lights, tossing my purse onto the hall table. It skidded and hit the little jewelry box, knocking it to the floor.

Fran picked it up and handed it to me.

I shivered as my fingers touched it. "Mr. Kamara gave

this to me to thank me for saving his life." I shivered
again and wailed, "Oh, Fran!"

"Now, don't get undone," Fran said. "Let's see what's
in here." He took the box away from me and pulled out
the cloisonné locket. "Very pretty. What's inside?"

"A movie-star picture."

"Are you a groupie?"

"No. I haven't even looked inside. Mr. Kamara told me
there was a picture of a movie star inside the locket."

Fran popped the locket open. "Dolly Parton? You
don't want to carry around Dolly Parton's picture, do
you?"

I had to laugh. "Of course not."

"I'll take it out for you. Then your locket will be ready
for someone else's picture."

He looked at me so archly I quickly looked away.
Didn't he ever give up?

"Whoops!" Fran said as the rim in the frame suddenly
gave way under the pressure of his fingernail. The rim,
the small oval sheet of plastic, and the picture suddenly
popped out and fell to the floor, along with a tiny, wad-
ded square of paper.

"What's that?" I asked. We both knelt on the floor.
Fran picked up the pieces of the locket that had dropped,
and I unfolded the small square of thin paper.

Fran's chin was on my shoulder, and his warm breath
was in my ear, as he tried to read the tiny handwriting on
the paper. I moved a little closer to him, just to make it
easier for him to read.

"It's a list of six names, with dates and cities," I said.

"What's it doing in the locket?" Fran asked. He put an
arm around my shoulders to steady me.

"Mr. Kamara must have put it there. But why?" I remembered the strange look of triumph on Mr. Kamara's

face and added, "I think this list was something he wanted to get rid of."

"So the next question," Fran said, "is why did he want to get rid of it?"

I sat back against Fran, trying to think, and the idea that burst into my mind terrified me. "Fran," I whispered, "Mr. Kamara must have been hiding this from someone."

Fran's lips nuzzled my cheek. "Then maybe we'd better find that person."

"I hope we don't!" I said. "I think that person is the one who murdered Mr. Kamara!"

12

The telephone rang, startling Fran and me so much that we both jumped up. "You'd better get it," he said. "It won't be for me."

It was my mother.

"Mary Elizabeth, sweetheart," she said accusingly, "you're still up."

"Of course I'm up, Mom. I just got home from work a few minutes ago," I said. Then I added, "Did you think you were going to wake me up?"

"I don't know when to call you," she answered. "When I call you at a reasonable time, you're asleep. So I thought I'd call you at an unreasonable time, and sure enough, you haven't even gone to bed yet."

"Have you?" This conversation didn't seem to be making sense.

"Your father and I went to a company party. We just got back to our hotel room. I thought I'd call and make sure that you're all right."

"I'm fine," I said.

"Are you remembering to bring in the newspaper and the mail?"

"Mom, I live here!"

"Oh, I know," she said. "I'm sorry I asked. Your father keeps telling me that you're a mature young woman, and he's right. It's silly of me to worry about you."

"Are you having fun, Mom?" I asked.

"Oh, yes," she said, "and meeting all sorts of nice people, which I'm sure you're doing too."

"You bet," I said. "Well, give my love to Dad. I love you, Mom."

"I love you, too, sweetheart," she said.

I put the receiver back in its cradle and said, "Good night, Fran. I'll see you tomorrow."

"I'll bring breakfast," he said.

"No," I told him. "Tomorrow I'm going to sleep late."

"Lunch, then," he said. "I'll pick up some hamburgers and fries. We can eat them before we go to the hotel. I can't stay and go home with you tomorrow night. My aunt and uncle are taking us to the Athens Bar and Grill. My uncle wants to try some Greek dancing." Fran made a face. "He doesn't dance very well in any language."

"Hamburgers will be great," I told Fran, and his eyes brightened. I looked again at the scrap of paper I still held. "Maybe if we talk about all this and share ideas, we can get a better idea of what's going on at the Ridley."

"Do you want me to take that paper with me?" he asked.

"No," I said. "I'm not afraid. I don't think that anyone but you knows I have it."

He hadn't moved, so I walked to the front door and opened it. My mind was on the list, so I was taken unaware when Fran reached up, pulled my head down, and kissed me good-night. It wasn't a quick kiss, and it wasn't a long, passionate kiss. It was one of those just-right kisses that are warm and soft and absolutely wonderful. I couldn't help enjoying it.

Finally Fran pulled away. "See you tomorrow," he said.

I shut the door and leaned against it, clamping my lips tightly together. They wouldn't stop overreacting. Why couldn't Fran be taller?

Somewhere, I told myself firmly, *there is someone just for you who is tall and gorgeous. Don't be so unhappy because Fran isn't.* I felt a lot better until I got the uncomfortable thought that somewhere just for Fran there was a girl who was short and beautiful. Darn! Life was just too complicated.

Before I went to bed I copied the information on that list and hid the copy under the mattress on my bed. Then I folded the paper just as it had been folded and put it back into the locket. I didn't have a picture to substitute for Dolly Parton's, so I put her back, too, complete with plastic and gold rim, snapping it all into place. It was too late to call Detective Jarvis and tell him about the list. I'd do it tomorrow—that is, later today. It was already tomorrow.

I slept with the bathroom and kitchen lights on and conducted the entire overture to *The Nutcracker Suite* before I fell asleep.

Sometime after the sun had come up, the ring of the telephone shot through my dream. I swam through the shattered pieces, reached for the receiver, and pulled it under the covers. I didn't even open my eyes. "Hello, Mom," I mumbled.

"It's not your mom. It's Tina."

"Mummmph," I said.

"I heard about your solving the problem of the stolen meat. Great work."

"Mummph."

"Lamar's going to station Nate out at the garbage bins tonight. Glad it's not me."

"Mummph."

"Anyhow, congratulations. I'll see you tomorrow."

I reached out and hung up the phone, immediately drifting back into my dream, which obligingly pulled itself together and went off in another direction.

Time doesn't exist in dreams, so I don't know how much of it passed before the telephone rang again. Once more I pulled the receiver under the covers and tried to mumble something.

This time it was Mr. Parmegan. He was brusque, clipped, and kept it short. That was fine with me. That meant I didn't have to say anything.

"I was apprised by Mr. Boudry about your work of detection last night," he said. "I'm thanking you by telephone, because with the number of appointments I have on my schedule for today, I would not be able to thank you in person."

"Thank you," I echoed.

"You're welcome," he said, and hung up. I did too.

I floated back into my warm, dark, comfortable place. When the telephone rang again I automatically brought the receiver in with me without coming to full consciousness.

"It's me—Art."

"Um-hmmm," I said.

"So what went on?"

"Why does everyone ask *me* about Soledat? Why don't they just talk to Lamar?" I murmured.

There was a pause. "I didn't get all the details," he said. "Fill me in."

"You know—tonight," I murmured, and tried to turn over without losing the phone.

Art said something else, but I tuned him out. "Good-night," I mumbled, and gave a gigantic yawn.

"Wake up," Art Mart said. "I'm talking to you. Remember, I'm your boss."

I groaned and tried to make myself think. "What time is it?"

"Eleven," Art said.

"Oh. Then I've got to get up anyway. Thanks for waking me up. Good-bye."

"Liz! Are you listening to me? Stop rambling on and answer my question."

I made myself sit up. That helped. Opening my eyes helped too. "What was the question?"

"Did anything happen in the club that I should know about?"

"Nothing."

"Then how come some of the stuff that belongs on the desk was scattered behind it on the floor?"

I told him about the drunk in the sauna. When I finished he said, "That's it? I thought you were going to tell me something important. You've just been wasting my time."

I growled into the telephone, but he'd already hung up. There's nothing like being angry to help you wake up. I stomped into the bathroom and washed my face and brushed my teeth. I remembered that Fran was coming over, so I put on my new yellow shorts and knit shirt. I wasn't wearing them for Fran. After all, he was just a casual friend. I was wearing them for myself. They were comfortable and cute and looked good with my red hair. Well, what was wrong with wearing them to please myself?

As I brushed my hair I wondered what was the matter with Lamar Boudry. He had practically sworn Fran and me to secrecy, then he ended up telling half the people in the hotel about Marco Soledat. I wouldn't be surprised if he hadn't notified Soledat himself.

I called Detective Jarvis from my bedside telephone, but he wasn't in. He had gone to Beaumont and would be back later in the day. I didn't leave a message, and I didn't want to talk to anyone else. I'd wait. Telling him about the list wasn't that urgent.

I had just walked into the kitchen when the doorbell rang. It was exactly twelve o'clock, and there was Fran with hamburgers, fries, and strawberry frosties.

"Great!" I told him. "I'm starving. But it's not fair for you to keep paying for our food. You bought the ice cream and the doughnuts too."

"You pick up the tab next time," he said.

"Okay." I popped a couple of fries in my mouth and licked the hot grease and salt from my fingers. "Next time, for a change, I'll get Mexican food. No. Wait a minute. Next time I'll make *fajitas*. I'm not much of a cook, but I make great *fajitas*."

We smiled at each other over our hamburgers. We were both so hungry that we didn't say much until we had almost finished our strawberry frosties.

"I'm looking forward to the symphony tomorrow night," I said.

"Speaking of symphonies"—Fran reached across the table and, with his napkin, wiped off my strawberry moustache—"I think you were right in the first place about all the crimes being orchestrated."

"I couldn't have been. You saw the deal with the stolen meat. A one-man operation."

Fran was smugly pleased with himself. "Think about it.

When did Soledat pick up the meat he had hidden in the garbage?"

"After he went off duty."

"Nope," Fran said. "His shift ends about the same time mine does, and I'm through about fifteen minutes before you. But Soledat didn't pick up his meat packages until after you and Tina would have left. Both times you saw him, you had stayed later than usual."

"Couldn't he have timed our schedule himself?"

"Too complicated. There are a lot of people involved. Soon after you leave, the night cleaning crew comes on, and so forth."

"So you think someone gave him the schedule."

"I think it's highly possible."

"But who?"

"Who would know the schedules?"

"Well," I said, "Mr. Parmegan would, and Lamar—" I stopped and stared at Fran. "Couldn't anyone get hold of a schedule? They must be written and in someone's office."

"Sure," he answered, "as long as it was someone with some kind of authority."

"Well, it can't be Lamar!" I said firmly. "Have you got any other good ideas?"

"Do you have some paper and a ballpoint?" he asked.

I got up and fished some out of the drawer under the wall phone in the kitchen. Fran began writing, and I slipped into the chair next to him and leaned over his shoulder so I could see what he was doing.

"You've drawn four circles."

"Same old circles," he said. "Maybe they can help us work this out."

"When we did this before I put a box where the conductor would stand and put a *K* for Mr. Kamara in it."

"This time let's put a question mark in the box," Fran said as he wrote.

I leaned closer, peering at the sheet of paper. "Your question mark looks like a *P*."

"I didn't promise calligraphy," he said. "You'll have to take what you get. Now—first circle in the orchestra: *meat*. We'll write *Soledat* on the line from the box to the circle." Fran leered and twirled an invisible moustache. "He'll soon learn to play another tune."

I groaned and sat back. "That's awful. Besides, we've got that one figured out. Go on to the sofa."

"It would be more comfortable than this kitchen chair."

"Fran, be serious."

"Whose name do we write on this line?" Fran said.

"That's a tough one." The room was quiet and filled with the warm, cozy pungency of onion and mustard. A fat black bee buzzed and batted against the window, and I could imagine my thoughts buzzing and batting inside my head, trying to form an idea.

"Who would need those sofas?" I finally asked.

"They'd never fit in a house," Fran said.

"A mansion, maybe."

"People who could afford a mansion wouldn't need to steal sofas for it."

"How about another hotel?"

"No good," Fran said. "A lot of travelers would come in and say, 'Oh, those are the sofas that were stolen from the Ridley.' "

"Not if they were re-covered. People would remember the fabric and color. A re-covered sofa would look very different. It's like when thieves steal a car they usually paint it another color."

He sat up straight and looked at the wall clock. "We've

got time. Let me make a few telephone calls. Where are your Yellow Pages? Look up the pages for upholstering companies."

Fran made one call after another. Each time someone answered he made his voice deeper and asked the same thing: "When are my two ten-foot sofas going to be ready?"

And after each answer he mumbled a quick "Sorry. I must have dialed the wrong number."

Until the fourteenth call. After his question and the answer that followed he snarled, "Who am I? You know who I am." There was a pause, and he said, "No, this is not your brother-in-law."

Fran hung up the phone and sat at the table again. He plopped his elbows on the table and rested his head on his hands. "Do you know how many small upholstery companies there are in Houston?"

"If I had stolen the sofas," I said, "I'd take them to a different city to be reupholstered."

Fran groaned. "This is harder than I thought it would be."

"Not for the police," I said. "That's one more thing I can tell Detective Jarvis about."

"One more thing? Oh, yeah. The list," Fran said. "He'd be the one to tell about it." Fran gleefully rubbed his hands together. "Are we on a roll, or are we on a roll! Sit down, Liz. Next up is the circle with *stolen items* in it."

I sat across from Fran. "None of the silver or paintings or things are taken through the doors of the hotel."

"Garbage again?"

"No. They'd have to be taken to the kitchen to be put into the garbage, and everyone in the kitchen would see them."

We both thought for a long time, until Fran said, "I think with this one we're up against a blank wall."

I bounced in my chair. "The wall, Fran! The gap in the wall. I know they're taken out through the wall."

"Then they'd have to be taken into the health club. People would see the things carried in."

"Unless they're smuggled in."

"Not many people could smuggle a painting under a bathing suit."

"Very funny."

"Listen," Fran said. "Other things must come into the club. Room service, for instance."

"Sure," I said. "Food. People are always ordering food and drinks. But no one brings in silver pitchers or paintings. Believe me, I'd notice."

"Is anything else brought into the club?"

"The custodians come in to clean it."

"There'd be a constant check on the custodians. That wouldn't work."

I leaned back and sighed. "Also, where would they hide the stuff? The only place in the health club would be the closet or the desk, and Deeley or I would see anything that didn't belong in either of those places. I think we'd better move on to the last circle."

Fran had written *wallet* inside the circle. "I think we know a lot more about this operation than we did," he said.

"We do?"

"Think about it." He squeaked his chair back from the table and tilted it. "Some of the cards were missing, then put back. You suspected that while the cards were out of the file the people on those cards had their wallets stolen by a pickpocket. You know of that one case—that Franklin Kurtin Quaiser."

"That's Kurt Quentin Fraiser."

"Whatever. According to Detective Jarvis, C. L. Jones was a known pickpocket."

"And every day he came to the club and talked to Mr. Kamara."

"Who else did Jones talk to?"

"Nobody, that I know of."

"Who else did Mr. Kamara talk to?"

"Nobody, except room service, when he ordered something to eat."

"Didn't Floyd Parmlee always bring his order?"

I jumped up and walked back and forth, so excited I couldn't stand it. "Yes! And I saw Mr. Kamara give him money! So Floyd could fit into the scheme!"

Fran's chair nearly went over backward. He grabbed the table edge, righted himself, and got up. "Listen, Liz, how about this? Floyd would be in a position to know who some of the big spenders were or who might open a fat wallet. Suppose he passed on that information to Mr. Kamara, who passed it on with the photo-ID cards to Mr. Jones? Then, after Mr. Jones stole the money, the three of them split it?"

"We've got it!" I said. I grabbed Fran and hugged him.

He hugged me back, and I suppose we could have enjoyed the hug for a while longer, except that he said, "But how did they get the cards from the file in the health-club office?"

I pulled back. "I don't know the answer to that."

"So what do we do next?"

I glanced up at the clock. "Let's go to the health club. We'll have a little over half an hour before we have to be on our jobs. Maybe we could look around. Maybe we'll get an idea."

I ran into the bedroom and pulled on my pink club

T-shirt and shorts and rejoined Fran. "How's that for fast?" I asked him.

"Fine," he said, "except you put your shirt on backward." So I had to go back into the bedroom and switch it around.

I began to put the box with the locket in it into my plastic purse, then changed my mind. "I'd better wear it," I said. "I could tuck it down under the neck of my T-shirt."

"The chain would show," Fran said.

"I know what I'll do." I took the locket out of the box and stuffed it into the hip pocket of my shorts. The T-shirt hung over the pocket, covering it nicely.

"Is anyone going to be upset at our nosing around?" Fran asked.

"Deeley won't care," I said.

And she didn't. "You want to show your friend around the club, be my guest," Deeley said, answering the excuse I'd given her.

"I'll just take a look through the men's side," Fran said, and went off murmuring, "Very nice, very nice."

"How's everything going?" I asked Deeley.

"Okay. Someone came and fixed the lock on the desk. You can put your purse in here again."

"Where's Art Mart?"

"Went off for more towels. We ran out real fast this morning. Had a big crowd."

Fran came back looking puzzled. "Nothing," he mumbled to me.

Deeley looked surprised. "It's not that bad. In fact, the guests think it's pretty nice."

"Well, it's got a great closet," Fran said, opening the extra door in the office and poking his head inside.

"Hey!" Deeley called. "That's not for the guests. That's just our supplies closet."

"Don't mind him," I said to Deeley. "He's just nosy."

"Open shelves, everything out in the open," Fran said. He closed the door.

Deeley was watching him suspiciously, so I said, "Come on, Fran. Let's sit by the pool and think—uh—talk."

We walked toward a pair of chairs that were under the ficus tree next to the pool. "I can't figure it," Fran said. He flopped into one of the chairs, staring up at the tree. I sat in the other chair.

Suddenly Fran stiffened and clutched the arms of his chair. "Do you know that tree isn't real?" he asked.

"I thought you knew that."

He sat up and looked at the bark. Then he poked out a finger and touched it. "But this part is real."

"Mrs. Bandini explained it to me. Real trunk, fake leaves. Otherwise they'd be all over the pool."

Fran got to his feet. "What about the roots?" He poked at the bark chunks around the base of the tree. "Glued," he said. With his knuckles he wrapped on the large brass planter. It answered with a deep, ringing bong.

"I told you the tree is fake," I said.

Suddenly Fran gripped the trunk of the ficus with both hands and pulled up and sideways. The tree and the base swung upward, leaving a large cavity in the huge brass planter underneath.

13

"There it is," Fran said, as we leaned over and stared into the empty planter. "The hiding place."

Deeley called to us from the office doorway. "What are you two doing with that tree?"

Fran carefully lowered the ficus and its base back onto an inside rim that held it in place. "This tree needs a dentist," he said to Deeley. "Definitely has a cavity, maybe even needs a root canal."

Deeley frowned at him. "That's supposed to be a joke?"

"He has a strange sense of humor," I said to Deeley. I tried to act calm and composed, but inside I was jumping up and down with excitement.

Deeley went back into the office, and I said to Fran, "Now we can tell Lamar what we know."

"Not yet," he said. "We don't know enough. We're guessing that the stolen objects were hidden in the planter, but we don't know how they were taken from here. A silver platter could go through the pool, but it wouldn't help a painting."

"Anyone inside the club could walk out through the

doors in the glass wall. They open from inside even when they're locked. They just don't open from the outside for people trying to get in."

"So the thief could just walk out with the loot?"

I nodded eagerly. "Right around the pool and through the gap in the wall. Now, can we talk to Lamar?"

"One more thing," Fran said. "How was the stolen stuff brought in here?"

I leaned back in my chair. "Darned if I know."

The door from the hotel opened as Mrs. Bandini and Mrs. Larabee came in. Mrs. Bandini was carrying a box about a foot square in addition to her usual gym bag. They were dressed in almost identical purple jogging suits, and Mrs. Bandini had a green plaid scarf tied jauntily around her hair.

As soon as they spotted me they waved and yoo-hooed and bobbled toward us as fast as they could go. Their smiles grew even broader as they came to a stop. Fran and I got to our feet. I introduced him.

Mrs. Bandini included Fran in her smile. "I remember you. Room service," she said.

"That's right," Fran answered.

"You're a very nice boy. Pauly likes you," she said. Then she turned to me, her eyes sparkling. "I've got two surprises for you, Mary Elizabeth. The first one you can enjoy right now."

With great ceremony she put the box on the table and removed the lid. It was filled with homemade cookies, golden and crispy and rich with the fragrances of butter and vanilla.

"Wow!" Fran said.

"Try one! Right now!" Mrs. Bandini said to me. "I'm glad your young friend is here. He'll enjoy some too."

I wished she hadn't said that.

Fran winced, but it didn't stop him from reaching for a cookie. Under the bright light of her smile I tried a cookie too. It dissolved into soft, sugary explosions on my tongue.

"These are great!" I said. Fran didn't say anything. He was busy reaching for more cookies.

The door banged open and one of the deep towel carts pushed through, with Art Mart guiding it. The cart rattled over the tiles, coming to a stop by the office door.

Art looked over at us, checked the clock, and frowned because it was only ten until three and there was nothing he could complain about.

Mrs. Bandini waved him over. "Come have a cookie," she said. "Mary Elizabeth won't mind."

Art strolled over, looked at the cookies, and took one. "You made these, Liz?"

"Mrs. Bandini made them."

"But they're her cookies," Mrs. Bandini said, "because I gave them to her for a present. They're not as fancy as Mr. Kamara's present, but they're given with my fondest wishes."

Art glanced sideways at me, the cookie suspended halfway to his mouth. "Mr. Kamara's present?"

Mrs. Larabee, who had been quiet for too long and now saw a perfect opportunity to jump in, immediately said, "A lovely cloisonné locket on a gold chain. He gave it to her for saving his life."

I closed my eyes and stifled a groan.

"When was that?" Art asked.

Mrs. Larabee and Mrs. Bandini rushed to give him all the details.

"You're not wearing the locket," Art said to me. "Where is it?"

"It wouldn't look right to wear it at work with my

uniform," I said. I glanced at the clock. "And speaking of
uniforms, I'd better get to work. It's almost three
o'clock." I didn't want to show anyone the locket until I'd
talked to Detective Jarvis, especially a jerk like Art Mart.

Fran said, "I'll just take one more cookie for good luck,
and I'll see you later, Liz."

"But how about—"

"Later," he said. "Got to report to work on time."

Deeley stood in the office doorway, plastic purse in
hand, her eyes on me; so I thanked Mrs. Bandini again
for the cookies, picked up the box, and hurried to the
office. Art was right behind me. "Stack the towels on the
shelves right now," he said to me, "then call housekeeping for someone to pick up the cart."

"I'll just have a couple of cookies before I leave,"
Deeley said, and reached into the box. "I was afraid your
crazy friend was going to eat all of them."

"Fran isn't crazy," I said, wondering why I felt so de-
fensive. "He's nice."

"Any guy who fools around with the artificial trees,
and says they've got cavities, seems crazy to me."

"What are you talking about?" Art asked.

"That ficus tree next to the pool," Deeley said. "It's
come loose, I guess, and her friend was poking around
inside."

Art scowled at me. "He didn't break it, did he?"

"He didn't hurt anything," I said. I put the top on my
box of cookies before they all disappeared, tucked it on
the ledge behind me, and locked my purse in the bottom
drawer of the desk. "See you tomorrow," I said to Deeley.

"Bye," she answered, and left.

Art left too. I didn't ask if he'd be back. I was just glad
the old grouch was gone. I was getting nervous about

that locket and list in my hip pocket. I decided if I couldn't give them to Detective Jarvis, I'd give them to Lamar. Fran may have put Lamar on our list of suspects, but I didn't agree.

I dialed the security office, and Tina answered. "Lamar's out of the building," she said, then lowered her voice as she added, "Marco Soledat had lunch duty today, but he didn't show up for work. Lamar went to Soledat's address, and found he moved his things out. The apartment was rented furnished, so Soledat didn't have any trouble leaving in a hurry."

"He must have been tipped off," I said.

"Looks like it."

"It's Lamar's fault," I said. "He told too many people about it."

"He wouldn't do that," Tina began, but I interrupted her.

"Tina, some people are coming into the club, and I've got to take care of them. Will you ask Lamar to come here as soon as he gets back?"

"Sure," she said, "but why?"

"Just tell him it's important. Thanks." I hung up just as a group sauntered into the office with bathing suits over their arms.

I handed them towels from the cart, then put the rest of the towels on the closet shelves. The cart was deep, and I was almost out of breath from all that bending and stretching by the time the last towel was tucked into place. I stood there staring at the towel cart while something wiggled in the back of my mind. What? Why should the towel cart make me feel so uncomfortable? I couldn't answer my question, so I pushed the cart out of the path of traffic from the hotel to the health-club office. Things weren't working out as well as I had hoped they would.

For one thing, I was disappointed about Marco Soledat. Lamar should have known better than to talk about it so much.

Per instructions I called housekeeping to pick up the cart, then set off for my usual beat in the pool area. Mrs. Bandini grinned at me as I neared her. "I didn't tell you about my other surprise for you," she said. "It comes tomorrow."

"What is it?" I was beginning to be curious.

"My grandson Eric, who is very tall and very handsome. Didn't I tell you I wanted to get the two of you together? Well, Eric is very interested in meeting you, after hearing all about you and what a lovely girl you are. He told me he would like to come to the club with me and meet you."

I instinctively backed up so quickly, I almost fell into the pool. Meet Eric Canelli? It was the last thing in the world I wanted to do. Tall and handsome? Grandmothers are notoriously biased. I could imagine that Eric Canelli was even more horrible than his little brother. He'd had a few years more time to practice.

I smiled, mumbled something, and got back to work, wishing that Lamar would show up.

A few hours later, when the telephone rang, I grabbed for it eagerly. "Mr. Boudry?" I asked.

It decidedly wasn't Lamar Boudry. This voice was high pitched and screeched with excitement. It took a few moments for me to figure out who was speaking and what she was saying. "Mrs. Zellendorf."

"That's what I told you!"

"You said somebody is in our house?" I gulped and tried to breathe again.

"Somebody *was*," she said. *"Was."*

"Oh, no! Did he rob the house?" I was shaking and

couldn't stop. I clutched the receiver as though it were an anchor.

"You aren't paying attention. Listen. I saw someone in your bedroom, but I knew you weren't there, because I saw you leave for work. So I called the constable service. They came in two and a half minutes."

"Did they catch him?"

"No, but they scared him away. As far as we could figure out, he didn't have a chance to take anything."

"Was he some kind of a nut? Did he trash the house?"

"Did he what? Oh. You mean make a big mess? No, except in your bedroom, and how much he did and how much you might have done I have no way of telling. I had two teenaged girls, and I know how girls don't always clean up their rooms the way they should."

"Mrs. Zellendorf," I interrupted. My heart was beating loudly and I wanted to shout at her. "Are the police there? Should I come home?"

"No," she said. "The burglar cut a little pane of glass in the back door, but I've got someone coming out in a few minutes to fix it, and I called your parents and reached your mother, and they're taking an early flight home."

"Today? But they're supposed to come home Monday."

"Would you stay if your house was invaded?"

"No," I said, and then it occurred to me how much she had done. "Thank you, Mrs. Zellendorf. You were wonderful."

"Just being a good neighbor," she said modestly. "With so much crime in the world, we all have to look out for each other." I could hear pleasure override the excitement in her voice.

I put down the telephone with shaking fingers. I was

glad my parents were on their way home. I'd be afraid to go into the house alone. I had to sit still for a few minutes until I knew my knees would work right and my legs would hold me up. The thought of some strange person in my own bedroom frightened me.

Everyone in the club seemed to be happily entertaining themselves and each other, so I wasn't needed at the moment. I put in another call to the security office. Tina answered again.

"Lamar's not back yet," she said. "What's the problem? Can I help you?"

"No. Just tell him to come here when he gets in," I said, and hung up the phone.

I wished I could talk some more with Fran, but I might not see him for hours. I could feel the locket pressing against my hip. The content of that locket was driving me crazy.

Tina showed up in a few minutes, a few photo-ID cards in her hand. "It's light on weekends," she said. "All the convention guys have gone home." She sighed. "Wouldn't it be neat if some really good-looking guy joined the club and came in every day?"

I knew I could trust Tina. I had to tell someone. I had to get some advice.

"Tina," I said, "I've got something to give to Lamar."

"Cookies?" she asked. "I saw all of you on camera stuffing your faces."

"Want some?" I asked, to be polite.

"No thanks," she said. "I'm watching my figure."

"Tina," I stammered, "Mr. Kamara gave me a locket."

"I heard about that."

"And inside it was a picture of Dolly Parton."

"Do you expect me to get excited about that?"

"Wait a minute. Behind the picture Fran and I found a

folded-up scrap of paper, and on the paper was a list of names and some other stuff about dates and places. I tried to get hold of Detective Jarvis, but he's out of town, so I want to give that list to Lamar."

"Want me to take it to him?"

"No," I said, "I think I'd better give it to him myself."

"Where is the locket?"

I just stared at her. Suddenly I was afraid of everything and everybody. I couldn't answer.

"Anxiety attack," she said calmly. "You're wondering now if you should have told me about the list. You're worried about what the list is, because you've dramatized it out of proportion."

"You act as though it's not important."

"It probably isn't. The guy who packed Dolly Parton's pictures in row after row of lockets probably accidentally dropped it in yours and didn't notice. Maybe it's a list of his old friends or something from an appointment book."

"Maybe."

Tina took a few cookies—just to be sociable, she said— and left the club. I sat at the desk, studied, and filed the photo-ID cards.

On Saturday there wasn't such a rush near dinnertime. In fact, most people had plans for the evening and cleared out early. I hoped Fran would drop by, but he didn't. As it got closer and closer to eleven o'clock, I became more edgy.

Where was Lamar?

Two people stayed in the pool, and I was so glad to see them that I grinned and waved each time they glanced at the office window. I rushed through the inspection of the women's dressing-room area, nearly colliding with the woman swimmer as she came in to change.

"Leaving so early?" I asked.

She looked at me oddly. "I thought you'd have kicked us out by this time. It's already two minutes after eleven."

"Well, so it is." I chuckled and went back to the office to wait for them.

They came through the office almost together and said a quick good-night. I heard the door to the hotel corridor shut behind them.

I raced into the men's locker area, mumbling under my breath that I had to pick up more towels than there had been swimmers, and dashed back to the office. I removed my purse from the desk and tossed the desk keys into the top middle drawer. Taking a deep breath I turned off all the lights in the club and tried to lock the office door.

My fingers shook as I kept trying to put the key in upside down. I closed my eyes, leaning my head against the door, and made myself relax. Then calmly I inserted the key, turned it, and heard the familiar click of the lock sliding into place.

That wasn't all that I heard.

Slowly I turned around.

Summer moonlight drenched the outer pool, brightening a wake of ripples that followed the dark shape that sped toward me under the glass wall.

I turned too quickly, stumbled, lost my balance, and fell to my knees. I clawed and scrambled my way up, trying to run toward the door to the hotel.

There was a loud splash behind me, and I could hear a body shove up onto the tiles. I couldn't make it.

"What's the matter, Liz? Are you still afraid of the dark?"

I whirled to face Art Mart, then leaned against the wall in relief. "It's only you," I said. "You scared me to death.

I didn't even know you were here. Why didn't you tell me you were in the pool before I turned out the lights?"

"I didn't want to bother you," he said. He moved closer to me, bent over, and shook the water from his hair.

"Don't you want a towel?" I asked. I stepped toward the office door, unlocked it, and turned on the office light. He came into the office with me, took the towel on top of the stack by the door, and rubbed his face, hair, and shoulders.

"Have you looked inside your locket?" he asked. "The one Mr. Kamara gave you?"

I tried to take a step away from him, but the office was too small and Art Mart was between me and the door.

"What are you talking about?" I managed to ask.

"A list," he said. "I know it's got to be in there. Give me the locket and I'll show you."

"I can't. It's—it's at home."

"No, it isn't. Just the empty jewelry box on the table." He moved a step closer to me. "Give me the locket, Liz, and save yourself a lot of trouble."

He snatched my purse from my hand. It didn't take him long to see that the locket wasn't in my wallet.

"I gave the list to Lamar," I told him.

"That's not what I heard," he said.

"Tina told you?"

"Uh-uh. I overheard you talking to her." He chuckled. "You weren't very bright to do that."

I tried to distract him, hoping I could edge toward the open door. "What kind of a list is it?"

He snickered at a joke he thought only he could understand. "You might say it's a kind of membership list— yeah—for a club."

"You mean for a syndicate."

His eyes widened. "You know more than I suspected you did."

"Why do you want the list?"

"The bottom line is always money, isn't it?"

"Who's going to pay you for it?"

"The same guys who killed Jones because he took it."

Art shifted his weight to the balls of his feet, as though he was ready to move toward me, and I desperately asked another question. Maybe his ego would help me. "Mr. Jones didn't know whose wallet he was taking, did he?"

One eyebrow lifted. "You know that too?"

"So do the police." If I thought I'd frighten him, I was wrong, so I added, "Those syndicate men will kill you too!"

"Naw," he said. "I did them a favor. They thought they'd get the list when they killed Jones. They didn't know he had passed it on to Kamara."

"They killed Mr. Kamara!"

He didn't answer, but his eyes told me how wrong I was. I gasped. "You?"

"Kamara made his first mistake in telling me he had the list. His second was in refusing to give it to me."

I blurted out, "You conducted the orchestra, didn't you?"

"What orchestra? What are you talking about?"

"I figured out that Floyd told Mr. Kamara who the people with money were, and he passed the word to Mr. Jones. Now I know who gave them the photo-ID cards. You did."

He was still listening, so I began to move a half inch at a time toward the doorway, talking rapidly. "And Floyd —maybe other people in the hotel—used the club's towel cart to hide valuables in. You were the only one who brought the cart to the club in the mornings, before the club opened. You stashed the stolen things in the brass planter under that ficus tree. Then, after the club was closed and dark, someone—" I stopped, remembering. "It was you I saw in the pool, wasn't it? You came into the club through the gap in the wall and the pool and took away the things that had been stolen."

I pointed at the tree, and as he automatically turned to look, I sidled another inch toward the doorway.

"There are still things I don't know," I said. "I don't know who fenced the things for you. Maybe it was Mr. Kamara. And I don't know who stole the sofas, but the police will find them before they get reupholstered."

He gave a start. "How'd you work that one out?"

I moved one more inch. He hadn't seemed to notice. By this time I was practically babbling. "And I don't know why Lamar told you about setting a trap for Marco Soledat, but—"

Art grinned. "He didn't. You did."

"No, I didn't."

"You should be more careful what you say when you're sleepy."

I tried to dodge, but he took a long step toward me and grabbed me tightly. I wiggled and struggled until I heard Art exclaim, "So there it is!"

In one motion he ripped away the hip pocket of my shorts, grabbed the locket, and slammed me against the wall. He kept his sharp elbow pressed against my ribs as he opened the locket, tearing out the picture and unfolding the list.

He looked so pleased with himself that for an instant I had the wild hope that he'd let me go, but he gripped my shoulders, turning me and pushing me so that I stumbled ahead of him. He turned off the office light and shoved me to the edge of the swimming pool. At my feet lapped the deep black water.

"Let's go swimming, Liz," Art said.

"Let's not," a strong, deep voice called from the darkness.

Art whirled, dragging me against him, and hooked his right arm across my throat and chin.

Shapes rose and flung themselves toward us.

"Stay away!" Art yelled as he kept moving back along the edge of the pool.

With a rush all the lights in the club zapped away the dark, and I blinked, trying to adjust to the sudden brightness.

Lamar stood there and Detective Jarvis, who held a gun in his hand. Tina was behind them, eyes as wide as though she were at a horror movie.

"Stay away!" Art repeated.

"It's too late for you to make such a dramatic move, Mr. Martin," Detective Jarvis said.

"You're not going to get the list!" Art yelled at them. He tossed the crumpled paper into the pool. I could imagine the ink running and fading as the paper soaked in the chlorinated water.

Art's voice rose. I squirmed, and his arm was rough under my nose. I could smell the damp sourness of his fear. Or maybe it was my own fear. "If you get near me I'll break her neck," he said.

"No," I mumbled, and wanted to spit out the hair on his arm that brushed my tongue. Feeling more like a trapped animal than a human being, I instinctively opened my mouth as wide as I could and bit down on his arm with all of my strength.

I don't know what happened next. I was knocked aside so violently that I went flying into the pool. So did Art

Mart, they told me later, except my right foot clipped him under the chin, and he slammed into the tile edge, knocking himself cold.

I panicked and swam with all my strength to the other side of the pool. It was something like being in the water with a killer shark. All I wanted was out.

I struggled up the steps, and there was Tina, who hugged me even though I dripped cold water all over her. "Liz, you were wonderful! You were brave! How did you do that with your foot?"

"Do what?"

She hugged me again. "There you go," she said, "Already your subconscious is repressing the terrifying memory and forcing it from your conscious mind."

"I kicked him, didn't I?"

"That's right."

Over Tina's shoulder I could see the door open. Two very familiar people came into the club. "My mother's here," I said. "And my father."

"Oh, dear," Tina said. "I wish I had my degree and training. I don't know how to handle this one."

"Mary Elizabeth!" my mother shouted from behind Tina. "What is going on here?"

I ran to hold them tightly. "I'll tell you all about it," I said.

And, after we were finally home and I was wrapped snugly in my father's big terry-cloth robe and my mother's fuzzy sheepskin slippers, I did.

14

Having a day off didn't mean a thing. I had to go down-town to give all sorts of information to Detective Jarvis and someone from the district attorney's office and all sorts of other people. They were awfully glad I had copied the list. From what I overheard, those names were going to help them make a big drug bust sometime very soon. I suspected that the woman who said she was Mr. Kamara's sister might very well be included.

Art Mart wasn't so cocky now. He was spilling names of accomplices in the hotel thefts so fast it was as if someone had tapped into a leak in his brain.

I was glad it was all over, and glad that Fran was there with me.

They left us alone for a few minutes, and I leaned back in my chair. "How I Spent My Summer Vacation," I said.

Fran smiled. "Then you're supposed to write what you learned from it, like 'crime doesn't pay.'"

I thought about my week plus at the health club. "That's not all I learned, Fran. I've been discovering something kind of crazy. Most people want to be somebody else. Mrs. Bandini wants to look like the women

who lead exercise classes on TV. Lamar wants to be Clint
Eastwood. Tina wants to be an instantly rich psychologist. And you want to be ta—" I stopped too late. It
didn't come out right, and I didn't get a chance to try to
make it better.

Fran said, "Everyone except you, Liz."

"Everyone except me what?"

"You mentioned all the people who wish they were
someone else, but you're different. You wish other people would change to be the way *you* want them to be.
You've got some fantasy in your head, and it's all you can
see, so that you can't accept other people for who and
what they are."

Fran got up and walked out of the room. I didn't call
him back. I felt as though he had punched me. His words
were more painful than Art Mart's big ugly arm. Fran
didn't understand. I was trying to follow my father's
advice. I didn't really want other people to change to suit
me.

Yes, I did.

A sick pain poked around my stomach. Fran had really
hurt me. I didn't want to think about it any longer. I felt
horrible.

I knew what would comfort me. I closed my eyes, sat
up straight in my chair, and tried to imagine myself on
the podium at Jones Hall with the Houston Symphony
Orchestra before me, instruments tuned and ready, each
musician waiting for my command. The musicians were
like pieces in a puzzle, neatly in place, ready for me to
take charge and tell them what to do.

Is that why I wanted to be conductor of a symphony
orchestra? So I could make things happen the way I
wanted them to happen? To make people be the way I

wanted them to be? Fran was a terrific person, and I liked him, but I hadn't been able to accept him the way he was.

Fran was right.

I groaned, and the musicians, the instruments, and Jones Hall dissolved with a *poof.*

Detective Jarvis came back into the room and said, "Mary Elizabeth, we're going to take you and Francis back to the health club. The attorney from the DA's office wants to view the scene and have you point out a couple of things."

Fran and I didn't talk much in the car. Every time I thought about what he had said, I wanted to cry.

And when we arrived at the health club there was no time to talk, even if we had wanted to. Mrs. Bandini practically flew out of her chair and rushed to meet us. Mrs. Larabee was on her heels.

"We heard! We heard!" Mrs. Bandini shouted.

"Although we'll be glad to hear it again straight from you," Mrs. Larabee said.

"We'll need her for a few minutes," Detective Jarvis told them.

"It's all right," Mrs. Bandini said, graciously giving him permission. "As long as I have one minute in which to introduce her to my grandson, Eric Canelli."

"One minute," Detective Jarvis said, and he walked over to the office with the attorney. Fran just dropped into the nearest chair and stared at his shoes.

Mrs. Bandini motioned, and out of the pool climbed one of the most gorgeous guys I've ever seen. On a scale of one to ten, he was a thirty-five. His hair was black and thick, and his eyes were as blue as the pool when it's lit at night. His smile was straight out of a dentist's magazine. I looked up, up, up. He had to be six feet four. Mrs.

Bandini hadn't been lying. She hadn't even been exaggerating.

"Hi," he said to me. "I'm glad to meet you. They told us it was your day off, so we didn't think you'd come in."

"It's perfect that it's your day off," Mrs. Bandini said. "I'll make dinner reservations for all of us at Vargo's. Would you like that?"

"Oh, I'm sorry," I said, and tried to look at least a little bit sorry just to be polite. "I've got a date for tonight." I stepped next to Fran's chair, put a hand on his shoulder, and gripped it tightly.

"But—" Mrs. Bandini's mouth opened and stayed open.

"Okay," Eric said, "I'll see you around." He walked back to the pool and dived into the water. Another good thing about Eric Canelli. He wasn't slow to get a message.

Detective Jarvis motioned to us. Fran hopped up and took my hand. We hurried to join Jarvis in the health-club office, where he was explaining something to the attorney. I didn't care what they were talking about. I just cared that Fran was holding my hand as snugly as I was holding his.

Fran moved closer as we came to a halt, and murmured, "You turned that guy down for me?"

"He may be tall and handsome," I said, "but he's not you, Fran. And you're the one I want to be with."

The telephone rang. Everyone else seemed to be busy, so I automatically reached over and answered it.

"Liz!" Tina exploded into the phone. "There is the most fantastic hunk out there in the pool! He's unbelievable!"

"Do you want to meet him?" I asked. "Come down, and I'll introduce you."

I hung up as Detective Jarvis was saying, "If you don't mind, we'll leave the two of you alone here for a few minutes. We're going to get Mr. Boudry. We want him to be in on this."

"Not at all," Fran said, and after they left the office he whispered to me, "Ways of being alone with you is something I'm planning to work on."

I liked that. I was thinking exactly the same thing.

JOAN LOWERY NIXON is the author of more than sixty books for young readers, including *The Kidnapping of Christina Lattimore, The Séance, The Specter,* and *A Deadly Game of Magic* (all available in Dell Laurel-Leaf editions), *The Ghosts of Now, The Stalker,* and most recently, *The Other Side of Dark.*

The Kidnapping of Christina Lattimore, The Séance, and *The Other Side of Dark* won the Edgar Allan Poe Award for the best juvenile mystery of the year. Ms. Nixon is the only juvenile book author to win three Edgars in this category. She has served as regional vice-president for the Southwest Chapter of the Mystery Writers of America.

Ms. Nixon lives in Houston with her husband.